ALONE ON
WITCH WORLD

She had been a lady, clothed in silk and gold—until the invaders came and laid waste to High Hallack. Now she wandered the desolate wilderness, her only companion a hunting cat, her only hope survival.

But then, in a deserted keep, two strangers appear: a young squire and his master, a man whose wandering wits have brought him all the way from the edge of a fatal battle, back across the painful miles to the origin of a legend. And despite her ever-growing fear, Brixia finds herself drawn inexorably into that web of ancient mystery.

The Witch World Series

WITCH WORLD	WARLOCK OF THE WITCH WORLD
WEB OF THE WITCH WORLD	SORCERESS OF THE WITCH WORLD
YEAR OF THE UNICORN	TREY OF SWORDS
THREE AGAINST THE WITCH WORLD	ZARSTHOR'S BANE

Other Ace Books by Andre Norton

BREED TO COME	ORDEAL IN OTHERWHERE
CROSSROADS OF TIME	PLAGUE SHIP
THE DEFIANT AGENTS	QUEST CROSSTIME
DRAGON MAGIC	RED HART MAGIC
THE EYE OF THE MONSTER	SARGASSO OF SPACE
FORERUNNER FORAY	SECRET OF THE LOST RACE
GALACTIC DERELICT	STAR BORN
ICE CROWN	STAR HUNTER/VOODOO PLANET
IRON CAGE	THE STARS ARE OURS
KEY OUT OF TIME	STORM OVER WARLOCK
KNAVE OF DREAMS	THE TIME TRADERS
LAVENDER GREEN MAGIC	VOORLOPER
MOON OF THREE RINGS	THE ZERO STONE

ANDRE NORTON

ZARSTHOR'S BANE

Illustrated by Evan TenBroeck Steadman

ACE FANTASY BOOKS
NEW YORK

ZARSTHOR'S BANE

An Ace Fantasy Book / published by arrangement with
the author

PRINTING HISTORY
Ace Original / November 1978
Third printing / July 1983

ISBN: 0-441-95491-X

Ace Fantasy Books are published by Charter Communications, Inc.,
200 Madison Avenue, New York, New York 10016.
PRINTED IN THE UNITED STATES OF AMERICA

1

WAN SUNLIGHT touched the upper reaches of this unnamed western dale to which Brixia's unguided wandering had brought her. It was far enough from the ravaged lands eastward to promise a breathing space of dubious safety—if one took care. Squatting on her heels, the girl grimaced at distant clouds to the east, a hint of worse weather to come. She drew the thin blade of her knife back and forth across the sharpening stone, eyeing that sliver of worn steel anxiously. It had been sharpened so many times and, though it had been well forged and strong, its making was in the past—the past she did not even try to remember nowadays. She had to be very careful, she knew, or that finger of metal might snap, leaving her with no tool— nor weapon—at all.

Her hands were sunbrowned and scarred, the nails of her fingers broken, rimmed with a grime which even scrubbing with sand could not banish entirely. It was very hard to think now that once all she had held was the spindle of a spinner, or the shuttle of a weaver, the needle of one who wrought pictures in colored threads upon the thick stuff meant to cover the walls of a keep. Another girl had known that living, soft and secure, in the High Hallack before the invaders came. Someone who had died during the time stretching behind her like a corridor, the far end of which was so faint in her mind that she had difficulty remembering.

That Brixia had survived flight from that enemy besieged keep which had always been her home made her as tough and enduring as the metal she now held. She had learned that time meant one day to be faced from sunrise until she could find some shelter in the coming of dark. There were no feast days, no naming of one month upon another—only times of heat, and times of cold when her very bones ached and sometimes she coughed and knew the bite of the chill until she felt she would never be warm again.

There was little spare flesh on her now; she was as lean and strong as a bow cord. And near, in her own way, as deadly. That she had once gone in fine wool, with a necklet of amber, and the pale western gold in rings upon her fingers—to her that now seemed like a dream—a troublesome dream.

She had walked with fear until it had become a familiar friend, and, had it been banished from her side, she would have felt queerly naked and lost. There had been times when she had nearly shut her eyes upon the rock walls of a cave, or upon the branches of some tree arched above her, ready to lose her stubborn will to endure, to accept death which followed her like a hound on the trail of a fal-deer already wounded by the hunter.

Still there was within her that core of determination which was the heritage of her House—was she not of of the blood of Torgus? And all in the south dales of

High Hallack had known the Song of Torgus and his victory over the Power of Llan's Stone. Torgus' House might not be great in lands or wealth, but in spirit and strength it must be reckoned very high indeed.

She raised a hand to brush back a wandering strand of her sun-bleached hair, sawn off raggedly at her neck level. Not for any skulker of the unsettled lands were the gold braided strands of a bower dweller. Now as she drew the knife back and forth across the stone she hummed the Challenge of Llan on so low a note that none but her own ear might have picked up that thread of sound. There were none to hear—she had scouted this place well shortly after dawn. Unless one counted as listener the black-plumaged bird which croaked menacingly from the top of a nearby, winter-twisted tree.

"So—so—" she tested the keenness of the blade on that errant strand of hair which kept fluttering down into her eyes. The sharpened steel sliced easily through the strees, leaving a puff of severed hairs between her fingers. She loosed her hold and the wind swept those from her. Then she knew a touch of fear again. Better—in this country unknown to her—that she had safely buried that portion of herself. There were old tales—that powers beyond the reckoning of her own people could seize upon hair, nails, the spittle from one's mouth and use such for the making of ill magic.

Save that there were none here, she thought, to be feared. Evidences there were, this close to the Waste, of those who had once held this country—the Old Ones. They had left monoliths of stone, strange places which beckoned or warned the spirit.

But those were but the markers of long vanished power or powers. And those who had wrought with such were long since gone. The black bird, as if to deny that, cried again its harsh call.

"Ha, black one," the girl broke off her hum to glance at the bird. "Be not so bold. Would you take sword against Uta?" Sitting back on her heels, she pursed her lips to give a low but carrying whistle.

The bird squawked fiercely as if it well knew whom she so summoned. Then it arose to swoop down slope, skimming only a little above the ground.

From the tussocks of green grass (there were no more sheep on these hills to nibble it ground short) there arose a furred head. Lips drawn back, the cat spat, eyes slitted in annoyance as the bird sheered off and was gone with a last croak of threat.

With the vast dignity of her kind the cat trotted on up to Brixia. The girl raised a palm in greeting. They had been trail comrades and bed mates now for a long time and she was inwardly flattered that Uta had chosen to company her so during her aimless wanderings.

"Was the hunting good?" she asked the cat who had now seated herself an arm's distance away to give close attention to the tongue washing of a back leg. "Or did the rats move on when there were no more people in that ruin to bring in food for them to steal?" Talking with Uta gave her her only chance to use her voice during this wary solitary wandering.

Settling back, Brixia surveyed the buildings below. Judging by the remains this had once been a well cultivated dale. The fortified manor with its adjacent defense tower—though now roofless, bearing signs of fire on its crumbling walls—must once have been snug enough. She could count twenty fieldmen's cottages (mostly from the outlines of their walls alone for that was all which remained to be seen) plus a larger heap of tumbled stone which might have been an inn. A road made a ribbon along which those cottages had been strung. It had run, Brixia guessed, straight to the nearest river port. Any traders coming into these upper dales must have followed that way. In addition those

strange and only partly tolerated people who roamed the Waste, prospecting in the places of the Old Ones, would have found this a convenient market place for their discoveries.

She did not know what name those who had lived here had given their settlement. Nor could she more than guess what had happened to turn it into the wasteland. The invaders who had ravaged all High Hallack during the war could not have reached so inland a place. But the war itself had spawned evil which was neither invader nor Dale, but born of both.

During that time when the Dalesman's levies had been called elsewhere, two-legged wolves—the outlaws of the Waste—pillaged and destroyed at will. Brixia did not doubt that when she went poking below she would find disturbing evidence of how this settlement had died. It had been looted—perhaps even the ruins combed more than once. She was not the only sulker in the wasteways. Still she could always hope that there remained something usable—if it were only a battered mug.

Brixia wiped her hands across her thighs, noting with a small frown that the stuff of her breeches was so thin over one knee that flesh showed palely through. Long since she had put aside skirted robe for the greater ease of a forest runner's wear. She kept her knife in her hand as she reached out for her other weapon, the stout hunting spear. Its point had been newly sharpened also, and she knew well how to use it.

Her pack she would leave here hidden in the brush. There was no need to linger long in the ruins, in fact perhaps she was wasting time to even explore. But Uta would have given her warning if anything larger than a rat or a meadow-leaper laired there, and she could always hope for a find. Her spear had come out of another just such blasted keep.

Though the dale, as far as she could see, seemed deserted, Brixia still moved with caution. There might be unpleasant surprises in any unknown territory. Her life for the past three years taught her the very slim edge which lay between life and death.

She closed her mind firmly on the past. It was weakening for the spirit to try and remember how it was once. To live for this day only was what kept one sane and alert. That she did live and had reached this place unharmed was, she thought, a matter for self congratulation. The fact that once she had known such a keep as home, worn soft wool, fancifully woven and dyed, over her now muscular and famine thinned body, no longer mattered. Even the clothes she now had were looted—

Those breeches, worn so thin, were of coarse and harsh material, her jerkin was of leaper skin, cured crudely, then laced together by her own hands, the shirt under she had found in the pack of a dead Dalesman, she having come upon the site of an outlaw ambush. The Dalesman had taken his enemies with him. She wore the shirt as she made herself believe as a gift of a brave man. Her feet were bare, though she had a pair of wooden-soled sandals in her pack, ready for the harder trails. Her soles were tough and thick, the nails on her toes rough and broken.

Her hair sprung from her scalp in an unruly, wiry mass, for she had no comb but her fingers. Once it had been the color of apple-ale at its most potent, sleek, shining, braided. Now, bleached by the sun, it looked more like autumn-killed grass. But she no longer possessed any pride in her person, only that she was strong and clever enough to survive.

Uta, Brixia thought fleetingly, as she slipped from one stand of brush and tree to the next (ever alert to any warning, ear, eye or nose might give), was far better named "lady" now. She was large for a house cat. But it might well be that she had never warmed herself before any man-set fire—being feral from birth. Only then her calm uniting with Brixia would be doubly strange.

Brixia had awakened from very uneasy slumber one night near a year gone, as far as she could reckon, though she kept no calendar, to discover Uta seated by her fire, the cat's eyes reflecting the light like large reddish coins in the air. Brixia had sheltered then in

one of the moss-grown, roofless husks of some building the Old Ones had left. She had discovered that
those drifters she must name enemy had little liking for
such relics. But there had been no harm in this one—
just walls fast returning into the earth.

She had been a little wary of Uta at that first meeting. But, save that the cat's unblinking stare made her
feel that she was being in some way weighed and
measured, there had been nothing remarkable about
Uta. Her fur was a deep gray, darker on the head,
paws and tail—with a blueish gleam when the sun
touched it. And that fur was as thick and soft as some
luxury cloth the traders had once brought from over-
seas in the lost years before the invaders' war tore the
dales from top to bottom, east to west, and broke life
apart into shattered pieces perhaps none of the sur-
vivors might ever gather together again.

In that dark face Uta's eyes were strange color,
sometimes blue, sometimes green, but always holding
a red spark by night. And those were knowing eyes.

Sometimes, when they were turned on Brixia, the girl had been uncomfortable—as at their first meeting—as if, behind the slitted pupils was an intelligence matching her own to study her in serene detachment.

Girl and cat, they now made their way to shrubs which formed an overgrown and untidy hedge-wall about the larger ruin Brixia had guessed to be an inn. Remains of two walls stood, fire marked and crumbling, no higher than the girl's shoulder. There was a cellar hole in the ground now near filled, and she had no mind to grub in that.

No—the best hunting ground was the lord's domain. Though that would have been the first to be looted, of course. Still if the fire had gotten out of control before the looters had finished, then—

Brixia's head went up. Her nostrils expanded to catch that scent. In the wilds she depended upon scent as did any of the animals, and, though she did not realize it, nor ever think about such things much, that sense was now far keener from constant use than it had been before war had made of her a rover.

Yes! Burning wood!

She dropped to hands and knees, crawled with a hunter's caution along the side of the inn, seeking a thinner place in that wall of brush which enclosed it. At length she lay flat, pushing forward the boar spear inch by inch, to lift back low-hanging branches and increase her field of vision.

Fire at this time of the year, when there had been no storm with lightning to set a spark, could only mark a camp of humans, Which in this country usually meant—outlaws. That some who had once lived here might have drifted back to see what could be salvaged— She considered that possibility and did not altogether dismiss it.

But even if the village Dalesmen had returned they could be her enemies now. They need only catch sight

of her for her to be their quarry. To their eyes in her
present ragged state she was no different than the
outlaws who had despoiled them before. They might
well take her for the scout of another such band.

Though Brixia searched the scene before her with
close attention she saw no signs of any camp. The
house was, she decided, too destroyed to provide
shelter. However, the tower still stood, and, though its
window slits were unshuttered to the wind and storms
and must have been so for a long time, the rest pre-
sented an appearance of being less ill used.

Whoever sheltered here must be in the tower. She
had no more than decided that when there was
movement in the doorway and someone advanced
into the open. Brixia tensed.

A boy—undersized—his fair head near as unkempt
as her own. But his clothing was whole and looked in
good condition. That was dark green breeches, boots,
and his jerkin was of metal rings sewed on to leather,
provided with sleeves to his wrists. He wore a sword
belt and, in the scabbard, a blade with a plain hilt.

As she watched, he threw back his head, put his
fingers to his lips and whistled. Uta stirred, and then,
before Brixia could stop her, the cat flashed out of
hiding and sped into the courtyard before the keep,
her tail banner high. But it was not she alone who
answered that summons. A horse trotted from around
the tower and came to the boy, dropping its head to
butt against his chest, while fingers scratched the root
of its forelock caressingly.

Uta had come into full view of the boy and now she
sat down, primly folding her tail end over her front
paws; turning on him, Brixia was sure, that same
measuring gaze which she used with the girl from time
to time. She, herself, was unwontedly irritated at the
desertion of the cat. For so long Uta had been her only
companion—Brixia had come to think of her as she

might a comrade of her own species. Yet now the cat had gone from under her very hand to visit with the stranger.

The girl's frown grew the sharper. There was nothing here for her—no chance to go searching for any useful loot. What remained, if anything did, would be discovered by this intruder. Best slip away as soon as she might and leave Uta to her fate. After all it looked as if the cat wished to change her allegiance.

The boy looked down at the cat. Now he loosed the horse and went to one knee, his hand outstretched.

"Pretty Lady—" he spoke with the accent of the

upper dales, and his words were startling to the listening girl. It had been so long since she had heard any voice except her own.

"Come—Lady—"

"Jartar?"

She saw the boy's body stiffen as he glanced back over his shoulder at the tower door.

"Jartar—" That other voice was low and there was something in it— Brixia crooked her arm to rest her chin as she lay in hiding—even her breath slow and light.

Two of them—at least. She had better not try to move yet—even though she was nearly sure that the craft she had learned by force of need was equal to covering any retreat.

The boy stood up, went back in the tower. With a toss of its head the horse ambled over the stone pavement, heading toward a good stand of grass. But Uta trotted toward that same doorless opening in the stone.

Brixia felt a small warmth of anger within her. They had so much—clothing, a sword, a horse—she had had nothing but Uta. Now it seemed she might even lose the cat. This was the time to get away. Still she made no move to slip back as quietly as she had come.

She had been alone for so long. While she knew that safety now lay only in loneliness, yet memory stirred. She watched the tower door with a certain wistfulness. The boy had not looked formidable. He wore a sword—but who in this land did not carry such weapons as he could find? Of late there was no law, no might of Dale lord to offer protection. Safety one carried in one's own hands, in the strength and dexterity of one's body. However, though she had heard only one voice calling out of the tower, that had the deep tone of a man's, it did not signify that there might not be more than one therein.

Prudence demanded that she creep away at once. Only—there was a need, born of a starvation of spirit, which was eating at her as might starvation of her spare body. She wanted to hear voices—see someone— Brixia had not known how deep was that desire until this moment.

Folly, Brixia told herself sternly. Yet she yielded to that folly, moment by moment. One of those moments proved her withdrawal already too late.

Movement in the door. Uta, who had reached the edge of that, withdrew by a graceful leap to the pavement without, sitting tail over paws again. Then the boy issued forth, but this time he half supported a companion.

A tall man, at least beside the boy he seemed tall. He walked oddly, shambling, his head bent forward as if he stared at the ground as he came. His arms swung loosely from his shoulders and, though, like the boy he wore mail (his being a well-made shirt of it—not crude ring and leather stuff), his belt scabbard held no sword.

He was wide of shoulder, narrow of waist and hip. His hair had been cropped, but not too recently, for it curled behind his ears and down a little on his neck, swept back from his sun browned forehead. That hair was very dark, and so were his brows which slanted upwards at the far corners. There was a cast to his features which Brixia's troubled memory noted. Once, a long time ago, she had seen such a man—

There had been a story about him—she groped for the first time in many months, deliberately stirring up memory she had sought to deaden. Yes! What had they said in whispers about that other man—a lord from the west who had spent a single night in the keep, sitting at meat in the high seat of an honored guest at her father's right hand? He was—half blood! Triumphantly her rusty memory produced the term she wanted—one of those the Dales folk looked upon

askance but trod softly about—one whose fathers had
wed strange ladies—people of the Old Ones—most of
whom had long ago left High Hallack, fading away
toward the north or west where no sensible man
would want to follow. There were always whispers
about the half-blood—they were said to have powers
which only they understood. But her father had welcomed that lord in open friendship and had seemed
honored that he stayed beneath their roof.

Now she saw that there *was* a difference between
that man in her blurred memory and this one who
came from the ruined tower. He did not raise his head
to look about him as he advanced a few steps, but
halted to stand quietly, still staring at the pavement.
There was a curious emptiness in his face. He had no
sign of beard (perhaps that also was a mark of his
ancestry) and his mouth opened slackly, though his
chin was well set. If it had not been for that emptiness
mirrored in his lack of all expression he might have
been considered a well-favored man.

The boy held him by the arm, drew him along, the
man obeying docilely and never looking up. Bringing
him to where there was a tumble of stones, his companion gently forced him to be seated there.

"It is a fair morning—" To Brixia's hearing the boy's
voice was strained, the words tumbled out too fast,
sounded too loud. "We are home at Eggarsdale, my
lord, truly at Eggarsdale—" The boy glanced about
him, glancing up and around as if he sought some aid.

"Jartar—" For the first time the man spoke. His
head came up, though there was no change in the dull
cast of his face as he called that word aloud. "Jartar—"

"Jartar is—gone, my lord." The boy caught at the
man's chin, strove to bring the slanted eyes up to meet
his own. Though the man's head moved unresistingly
in that hold, Brixia could see there was no change, no
lightening of the deadness in that set stare.

"We are home, my lord!" The boy's hands went to the man's shoulders, shook him.

The body in that hold yielded limply to the force of his shaking. Still the man did not resist, nor show that he recognized either boy, words, or the place in which he sat. With a sigh his young companion stepped back, again looking about the courtyard as if to summon up some aid which would break what lay upon his lord like a spell.

Then he knelt, took the man's hands in his, held them tightly against his breast.

"My lord," Brixia thought he used a vast effort to keep his voice even, "this is Eggarsdale." He formed each word slowly and distinctly, speaking as he might to one who was deaf but might hear a little if one took good care. "You are in your own place, my lord. We are safe, my lord. Your own safe place, you are home."

Uta arose, stretched, moved lightfooted across the pavement towards man and boy. Coming to the right side of the man she reared, setting her forepaws on his thigh to look up at him.

For the first time there was a change in that face so lacking in any sign of intelligence or emotion. The man's head turned slowly. He might have been fighting against an obstructing force in order to move at all. But he did not face the cat. The boy's visible surprise became demanding concentration, including both cat and man in the intentness of his gaze.

His lord's lips worked. The man might be fighting to produce words which he was unable to speak. For a long moment he continued so. Then he lost that measure of faint attention, if attention it had been. Once more his face emptied, was the mirror of a ruined mind, as broken as the remnants of what the boy had called his home.

Uta dropped from her place at his knee, eyed the

down winging of a butterfly, to bound away after that with playfulness she seldom displayed. The boy loosened the man's hands, sprang after the cat, but she skimmed neatly between his reaching hands, slipped away between two stones.

"Puss—puss!" He dodged around the stones, hunting and calling frenziedly, as if to regain sight of the cat were the most important thing in the world.

Brixia smiled wryly. She could have told him his efforts were in vain. Uta went her own way. The cat must have been curious about the people in the tower. Now that the curiosity was satisfied they might never see her again.

"Puss!" the boy pounded with his fist on top of part of the tumbled wall. "Puss! I—he *knew*, for a minute—by the Fangs of Oxtor, he knew!" He threw back his head and cried that last aloud like a battle shout. "Puss—he knew—you must come again—you must!"

Though he said that with all the intensity of a wise-woman evoking one of the Powers, he had no answer. Brixia realized what the boy wanted. That faint interest of the man in thè curious cat must mean a great deal to his companion. Maybe it was the first response his lord had shown to anything since wound or illness had reduced him to this husk. So the boy wanted Uta to hand as a hope—

Brixia stirred a little. So engrossed was that other in his own web of hopes and fears, she felt that he might rise to her feet and walk away in the open, without his noting her. And she should withdraw—only now a curiosity perhaps akin to Uta's kept her where she was. Though her wariness had eased a little—she saw in these two no immediate open threat to herself.

"Puss—" the boy's voice died away almost despairingly.

The man shifted a little and, as the boy turned

towards him, he raised his head. There was no change on his dead face, but he began to sing as a songsmith might voice a song for a hall feast.

"Down came the Power
  By Eldor cast—
Fierce pride,
  Strength meant to last.
Out of the dark
  At his call
Came that to make him
  Lord of all.
But Zarsthor bared the Sword of Mind
  Raised Will's shield,
Vowed by Death, heat and heart,
  Not to Yield.

Star Bane blazed,
  Grim and bright
Darkness triumphed
  Over Light,

Zarsthor's land fallow lies,
  His fields stark bare.
None may guess in aftertime
  Who held Lordship there.
Thus by the shame of
  Eldor's pride
Death and ruin came to ride.

The stars have swung—
  Is the time ripe
To face once more
  the force of night?
Who dares come in dark and shame
To test the force of Zarsthor's Bane?"

The poor verse might limp, sounding little better than the untutored riddling of an unlettered landman, yet there was something in his singing which made Brixia shiver. Zarsthor's Bane she had never heard of. However nearly every dale had its own legends and stories. Some never spread beyond the hills which encircled that particular holding. The boy halted. His incredulous expression once more became one of excited hope.

"Lord Marbon!"

Only his joyous hail had just the opposite effect. The man's vacant face once more turned downward. However, now his hands moved restlessly, plucking at the breast of his mail shirt.

"Lord Marbon!" the boy repeated.

The man's head turned a little to the right, as one who listened.

"Jartar—?"

"*NO!*" the boy's hands clenched into fists. "Jartar is *dead*. He has been dead and rotting this twelfth month and more! He is dead, dead, dead—do you hear me! He is dead!"

The last word echoed bleakly through the ruins.

2

IT WAS UTA who broke the silence following the dying away of that resounding and despairing word. The cat crouched to face that portion of the hedge behind which Brixia flattened in hiding. From her furred throat sounded what was near the scream of a a tormented woman. Brixia had heard such a shriek before—it was Uta's challenge. But that it was aimed at her came as a shock.

The boy whirled, his hand slapping down on the hilt of his sword in instant reaction. There was no chance now for Brixia to slip away—she had waited far too long. While to continue to lie here only to be routed out of hiding like the cowardly skulker they might well deem her— No! That she would not wait for.

She arose, pushed through a thin place in that hedging, to advance into the open, her spear ready in her hand. Since there was no arrow on any bow string to provide menace, she believed her spear was fair answer to the other's sword.

Uta had faced about after that betrayal, staring round-eyed at the boy. His face was taut, wary. Now his sword was out of the scabbard.

"Who are you?" There was wariness in his sharp demand also.

Her name would mean nothing to him. During the past months of solitary wandering it had come to mean little to her either. She was far from the dale of her birth, even from any territory where naming her House might have some proper identification. Since she had never heard of Eggarsdale it was logical to suppose that such an isolated western holding would never have heard in turn of Moorachdale or the House of Trogus which had ruled there before all ended in a day of blood and flame.

"A wanderer—" she began, then wondered if answering that demand at all would in a small way weaken her position.

"A woman!" He slapped his sword back into its sheath. "Are you of Shaver's get—or Hamel's—he had a daughter or two—"

Brixia stiffened. The tone of his voice— Pride she had forgotten made her stand straight. She might have the outward seeming of some field wench (which he had certainly deemed her by his manner) but she was herself—Brixia of Trogus' House. And where was that now? There was a ruin as smoke blackened and desolate as this—nothing else.

"I have no tie with this land," she said quietly, but her level return gaze was a challenge. "If you seek some field woman of your lord's holding—look elsewhere." She added no title of respect to that statement.

"Wolfhead wench!" The boy's lip curled. He drew back a step, taking his stand before his lord in a gesture of defense. His eyes darted right, then left, striving to seek who else might lie in concealment.

"Those are your words," she returned. It was as she had thought, he believed her one of an outlaw band. "Give not any name to another, youngling, until you are sure." Brixia put into that all she could summon of the proper distance-speech she had once known. A Lady of the Holding would speak so in answer to such impertinence.

He stared at her. But before he could reply, his lord moved, got to his feet. Over the boy's slightly hunched shoulder his dull eyes regarded the girl without interest, or perhaps even not seeing her at all.

"Jartar delays—" The man lifted one hand to his forehead. "Why does he not come? It is needful we be on the march before nooning—"

"Lord," his eyes still on the girl, the boy backed another step, putting his left hand on his lord's arm, "it is time to rest. You have been ill, later we shall ride—"

The man moved impatiently, shook off that touch.

"There will be no more resting—" a shadow of firmness deepened his voice. "There can be no resting until the deed is done, until we have the ancient power again. Jartar knows the way—where is he?"

"Lord, Jartar is—"

But though the boy once more grasped at the other's arm, the man paid no attention to him. There was again a shadow of awareness on his face, a lifting of that cloud of dull unreason. Uta trotted toward the pair of them, come to stand before the lord. Now the cat uttered a soft sound.

"Yes—" Exerting himself, the man pushed aside the boy, went to one knee on the pavement and held out both hands to the cat. "By Jartar's knowledge we can go, is it not so?" He asked that question, not of his human companion, but of the cat. His eyes met those of the animal with the same unblinking stare as Uta could focus for as long and steadily as she wished.

"You know also, furred one. Have you perhaps come as a sending?" The man nodded. "When Jartar is with us—then we shall go. Go—" The slight animation he had shown began to fail, knowledge slipped visibly away from him. He was like a man swiftly overcome by slumber he could not fight.

The boy caught at his shoulders.

"Lord—" He looked beyond the man he supported to the girl.

There was such hostility in the glare he turned upon her that Brixia took a stronger grip on her spear. It was as if he hated the sight of her enough to open attack. Then a flash of understanding came to her. He was moved by shame—shame that someone should see his lord so bereft of his senses.

Instinctively, at that moment, she also guessed that for her to make any sort of a move, say anything which would show she did understand, might in turn render matters worse. Totally at a loss Brixia met the boy's glare with what calm she could summon. She wet her lips with tongue tip, but said nothing.

For a very long moment they stood thus and then his glare became a twisted scowl.

"Get out! Go—! We have nothing left worth the stealing!" He made another gesture towards his sword.

Brixia's temper flared. Why that order seemed like a lash laid across her face she could not have told. These two were nothing to her. She had seen suffering and trouble enough, and had learned that in order to survive, she must go her own way—alone.

But she curbed that temper. With a shrug, she retreated toward the hedge from which she had emerged, caution telling her not to turn her back on the pair. Though she, nor no one else, need have anything to fear from the man.

The boy had him on his feet again, was urging him back towards the tower door with a steady murmur of encouragement pitched too low now for Brixia to hear. She watched them disappear before she went also.

It would be wise to leave the dale entirely, she told herself as she climbed the slope towards the ridge top. Yet she made no move to go. An expertly flung stone stunned one of the leapers in the grass, and she dressed the lean body skillfully, saving the skin to be worked upon at her leisure. Six such would form a short cloak and she had three already green cured and rolled within the journey bag at her hidden campsite.

Knowing that she might not be the only one to have marked those camped in the ruins, she took extra precautions at concealment herself. Had any outlaws seen the horse, the sword the boy wore—that would be loot enough to draw down a small raid. Brixia wondered if the boy realized how dangerous his camp among the forgotten hold buildings might really be. She shrugged. If he did not it was no responsibility of hers to correct that ignorance.

As she built her small fire of carefully selected wood which would give the least possible smoke, and then used a spark from her prized snapper to light it, her thoughts were with the two below. Brixia was reasonably sure there were only two.

The boy named this Eggarsdale and spoke of it as home. His Lord was plainly unable to care for himself—how then did they propose to exist? Yes, there was game of a sort to be found. But without a bow one had to have dexterity with a throwing stone to bring a leaper down. She had near starved—had eaten grubs and chewed on grass—until luck favored her and she had learned enough to remain alive. While a single leaper made hardly a full meal for one at best.

Brixia turned those bits of her own catch she had spitted in the heat of the fire, to be half cooked before she tore at them hungrily, and sat back on her heels. Though she had had no time to explore the long overgrown garden patches below she could well guess that few edible plants had seeded, or rerooted themselves during what was doubtless years of abandonment. There were herbs one could cull, and that she had done when and where she could. But those, if they could be found, would not show in any quanity. Unless those two had come supplied—how were they to fare?

Brixia turned her stick spits again, jealous of the fire which sputtered and leaped under the spill of juices she had no way of catching. Her mouth filled with saliva as she smelled the roasting meat.

There was a small sound to draw her attention to the opposite side of the fire.

"Unfriend," she said, eyeing Uta sternly. "If you have changed your House Shield, lady, then go there and ask for a guest place at the great table—come not to me." Still she flipped one of her meat sticks up, stripped its burden off, using a leaf to shield her fingers, letting the half-seared chunks lie on a second leaf for Uta to take or refuse.

The cat sat waiting for the meat to cool enough to mouth. Yet she glanced only now and then at the offering, rather watching Brixia the while in that disconcerting unblinking manner. The girl shifted. It was only Uta's way—there was no reason to feel that in some fashion her own thoughts were being combed and shifted.

"Yes, go to them, Uta. The big one seems to like you well enough."

The girl narrowed her own eyes and stared as straightly back at the cat. Uta's actions in regard to the man had puzzled her. Not for the first time she wished there was some way of communication possible between them. Before that desire had been born of her own loneliness—at those times when that had formed a prison for her. Then the physical presence of the cat had not been enough to banish the girl's dark thoughts, Brixia had longed for another voice—to shake her out of such aching emptiness.

Now she wished speech because of curiosity. In some way Uta had been able to pierce the clouded mind of this Lord Marbon—to bring him into some measure of awareness. Why—and how?

Brixia took up a skewer and waved it in the air, cooling the meat it impaled enough to chew at it.

"What did you do to him, Uta?" she asked. "He is as one moon-blasted. Did it come from a wound, I wonder, or some trick of the invaders? Perhaps a fever— Who is this Jartar upon whom he calls, and who the boy says is dead?" She chewed vigorously at the tough meat. Uta was eating, too, and had not even looked up at her questions.

That song—it could not be any of a swordsmith's making—crude, ill fashioned—like it had been done by someone without skill, only a driving purpose. Brixia was slightly surprised at the turn of her own thoughts. But to her those carried the sense of truth. Purpose in that song? Zarsthor's Bane—what else had the song named it? Star bane.

Someone called Zarsthor had taken up the sword against a foe and had been destroyed because the enemy had had this weapon. Brixia shook her head. There were legends in many about old wars and struggles. All of them held a small kernel of truth, but a truth which meant nothing today. Unless the dark touch of Zarsthor's Bane still lay upon this dale.

Nothing was entirely improbable among the dales of High Hallack. The Old Ones, before they had withdrawn from the lands bordering the great sea (fading

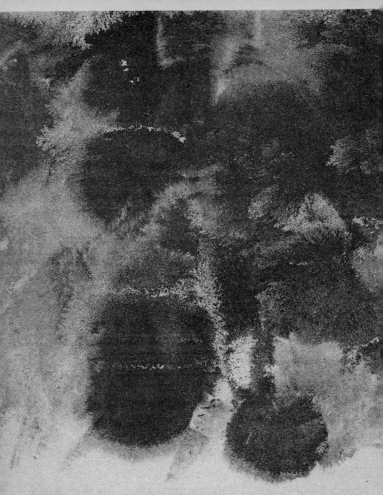

northward or westward beyond the Waste itself), had strange knowledge and many powers. There were places to be shunned and other places— She stopped eating as a sudden flash of memory struck her with such intensity that it was almost as if she herself had been whirled away in both time and distance.

The afternoon that they had fled from Moorachdale's keep, when the warning came that the defense could no longer hold, Brixia's breathing quickened. Running—running through the twilight— the soon-come leaping of destroying fire behind, the screams and shouts— It seemed that at this moment

she could feel again a sharp pain beneath her ribs, that
in her leg—as she fought against the drag of her long
skirt, fear sour in her mouth.

On—up to the ridge. Kuniggod had run beside her,
urging her on. Kuniggod— Brixia's face twisted at that
memory. She wanted to thrust it away from her—far
away—but memory would not now be denied.
Kuniggod, who had risen from her bed wheezing and
coughing from the Deep Chill, but who had made sure
her nurseling was out and away before death fought its
way to the door of the ladies' bower—using the inner
stair of the hall—the bolt hole gate.

They had run though the night, apart from any
others who had broken free. Thus Kuniggod had led
her to that narrow way among tall stones where they
had stumbled along, clinging to each other, Brixia then
half witless with fear. She had been so unkowing of the
way which they were taking that they had come into
that Place before she noted truly what was about
them.

No dalesblood willingly sought the sites which the
Old Ones had once claimed for their own purposes—
not unless such a seeker was a Wise Woman already
learned in some of the unwritten knowledge. Even
then that Wise Woman walked softly and with great
care, for there were malific powers to be faced—
sometimes rising without warning. Save that Brixia
had always heard it whispered that such plague spots
of the Dark had their own warning atmospheres and
could be smelled, or felt, before the foolish were full
into their nets.

Where Kuniggod had guided her was one of those
shunned places, yet it seemed that her old nurse had
had knowledge of it. For as she had sunk, coughing,
with tearing gasps for breath in between, the woman
had clutched at Brixia, holding her with all the strength

she could summon when the girl, coming to her senses, would have run forth again.

"Stay—" she had gasped. "This is—not—of—any evil—"

Then Kuniggod had fallen forward on her face so that Brixia had in turn knelt to gather her into her arms, hold her, while the woman choked and struggled for breath. The girl knew that her old nurse could go no farther, nor could she go on and leave her. So she had huddled under the glow of a moon which was far too full and bright—for it appeared to hang directly above them—showing her every detail of the place.

It did not form a true circle she perceived by a closer study. Rather stones of a silvery gray-white, which shimmered in this light, formed two crescents, their pointed horns some distance from each other— leaving so two entrances to the inner part where the refugees crouched. Those stones were not rough, rather had been smoothed before being set so. Brixia could see that there were lines traced near the top of each. But whether those formed some design, or were the remains of inscriptions too weather worn to be any longer read, the girl could not tell.

However, the longer she studied those stones the more the light appeared to curdle and cling about them. They might, to her fear dazzled eyes, be giant candles, their light exuding from the sides as well as from those crowns where wicks should have been. Yet the light in the stones did not spread far beyond them, only furnished a glow to cloak each pillar.

Looking upon those steady glimmers of light Brixia's first fear of the unknown had slowly seeped away. Her heart, which had pounded so fiercely as Kuniggod had drawn her here, slowed its beat. She began, without realizing, to breathe both more deeply and quietly. From somewhere came a numbing, a lassitude, which

oddly comforted her. Her head nodded, she felt pleasantly drowsy, content.

At length she must have slid down to lie, Kuniggod's head still pillowed on her arm, feeling as safe as if she rested behind the drawn curtains of her own bed. And so lying she fell gently into a deep sleep.

When Brixia had aroused the next morning she still lay with Kuniggod, and it had taken her time to realize where she was and what had happened to her. No stark fear returned to assail her. A curtain had dropped between her and what had happened the night

before—as if years of time separated one part of her
life from another. She had sensed a new strength, the
restlessness of purpose which she could not understand, but her ignorance did not bother her.

Nor had the girl felt more than a shadow of sorrow
when she knew that Kuniggod's spirit had left her.
Brixia had placed her nurse's hands together on that
quiet breast, kissed her forehead. Then she had stood
and looked at the pillars. In the light of morning they
were simple stone. Still there continued to abide in her
this peace, or an absence of emotion—a new freedom
from her fears. She knew then that it lay within her to
survive—that survival in fact was demanded of her for
a purpose which was not clear.

Whether that peace was of good or ill, she did not
question. In that dawn light it gave her the strength to
go on living, and enough of it she bore with her as
shield and support through what lay ahead.

Now in this camp above Eggarsdale Brixia sat gazing into the flames and wondering. What had worked
in her during that night she had spent encircled by the
double sign of the new moon? Why had that memory
now returned to her so exactly and in such vivid detail
at this moment when somehow she had never desired
to recall it before? Why did it seem that all which lay
before that hour was of very little account in her life,
rather that what she had done since had more
meaning—would be of use to her?

Why—and why—and why—?

"There are many whys," she said aloud to Uta. The
cat was washing her face, but at Brixia's words she
stopped the swing of her paw, looked over at the girl.

"I am Brixia of the House of Torgus—or am I still,
Uta? Oh, I do not mean the wearing of fine wool, the
sitting in a seat of honor, the saying to man and
woman—do this—and having it done. Those are not
the signs truly of House birth. Look upon me," she

laughed and was startled, realizing how long it had been since she had voiced such a sound. "I look as such as might beg meat from a feasting, or be stoned from a village by those minded not to treat with suspicious wanderers. Yet it is true, I am Brixia of the House of Torgus—and that only I myself can take from me—by some act so unworthy of my heritage that I must judge myself and render punishment thereafter.

"Your young friend in the valley rendered outward judgment upon me, Uta." She shook her head. "I thought I had thrown aside pride as a useless thing. Pride does not put food in the mouth, covering on the back, keep breath within one's body. Not that kind of pride. Perhaps I have rather the need to say 'you cannot defeat me—you shadow of fear!' That is the kind of pride you walk with, Uta. I think it is a good pride."

She nodded emphatically. Still in the girl stirred a core of discontent. She had remembered too much, even though it was clouded and far away. And how that boy had looked at her—that now began to sting more than it had even when it first touched her.

"So be it!" Brixia balled her right hand into a fist and drove that into the cup of her left palm. "Those two are nothing to me, Uta. Nor can their thoughts touch me now. We shall be off with the morning coming and leave them to lord it over their tumbled blocks of stone."

What she said was the best of good sense. Still—

As Brixia went about making her preparations for a night's camp—finding a break in the ridge which was nearly half a cave and covering its floor with dried leaves and grass for the kind of nest she had come to use for her temporary lodging places, she paused now and then to glance at the tower below. Now she did not skulk or attempt to conceal her presence. For she was sure that the boy had no reason to seek her out, his care for his lord would occupy him fully.

She watched him come from the tower, take the horse to where a stream ran. After the animal had drunk, he led it back into a walled field. Then he went again to the stream side, bringing along a leather saddle bottle which he filled and carried back to the tower. Never did he look up, she might already be wiped from his mind.

Somehow, that, too, was like a prick against tender skin. Though why she should care, Brixia did not understand. His unconcern made her more bold. She took no cover as she herself went to that stream with her own worn water carrier. And she lingered to wash her face and her neck, wishing that there was a pool hereabouts which she could use for a mirror. Though perhaps it was just as well there was not, she decided as she combed through her thatch of hair with her fingers, picking out bits of leaf and twig left by her journey through the hedge.

Why she lingered—even arranged to camp here for the night—Brixia could not understand. Her stay had no purpose, yet, when she tried to plan going on, there was an uneasiness in her which would not let her leave that bed for far. Restlessly she prowled along the ridge above. Even when she, almost absentmindedly, brought down another leaper she took no pleasure in her skill or such excellent unexpected addition to her supplies.

When Brixia returned to her nest place, she found Uta crouched on the crown of one of the rocks which formed its sides—the cat's head fixed so that she looked, not down at the tower, but rather along the ridge itself to the westward where the dale opened its other throat upon the dreaded Waste.

"What is it?" Brixia had seen that concentration in

Uta before, and she had fast learned what it might well portend.

Though the girl's senses, trained by the life as she was following, were keener than most of her kind, they were sadly limited compared to the cat's. Brixia raised her head, used sight and her sense of smell, as well as hearing, for the task of finding what was serious enough to keep Uta so absorbed.

There was a trail of smoke from one vent in the tower. Those sheltering there apparently did not know the trick of picking the right dried wood to give as little sign of a fire as possible, or else they did not care if their occupation was noticed. No, not the Keep—then—

The girl dropped down in the shadow of the rocks, staying on her knees, the standing stone favored by Uta pressing against her left shoulder, exposing as little of her body as she could while she surveyed the dale. There were the broken walls which had marked the fields, the gardens, and the crop places. Brush made a thin screen, spreading ever farther, along some of those walls. To the west the fields ended in a copse of wood which no sight, unless it be that of a bird, could penetrate.

But up out of that wood now burst birds. Those wheeled and called hoarsely. Brixia snatched up her spear. She knew meaning of such alarm signs very well. There was an intruder in the woods—and these birds had very little to fear save—man!

Intruders—coming out of the waste? Had they been of the same party as the two below surely they would have ridden in from the east following the old road. Outlaws—rats and wolves from the Waste gathering to gain what scant pickings might still lie here—even as she had earlier thought to comb the ruins.

Rats and wolves they might be—but they had fangs and claws!

A boy with a sword—a man with blasted wits—and neither given any warning.

The two were nothing to her. And what had she—a knife thinned near to the point of breaking when she put any pressure on it—a hunting spear? It would be folly—rank folly—

Her thoughts hammered at her. But she was already slipping away from her hiding hole, heading down slope, using every fraction of cover craft she knew. Beside her Uta crept with the same caution.

This act was folly, but somehow she was bound to it.

KNOWING WELL that the tower must already be under
observation by those hiding in the wood which lay in
the opposite direction from the way she herself had
taken, Brixia crouched in the last bit of cover consider-
ing her next move. It was plain she must come into the
open in order to reach that shadowed door. If she were
only Uta now—

Uta! A furry head nudged against her arm and she
glanced at the cat who eyed her intently in return.
Then Uta moved to the right, melting in her own way
into the tangle of brush. Perforce Brixia went on hands
and knees after her, struggling to force a path through
that mat of vegetation.

Stone broke the wall of brush—the foot of the wall
which had once been the outer defense of the keep. It
was roughly laid, one unsmoothed block placed upon
another. Uta used it as a ladder, climbing from one
pawhold to the next on her way to the top.

Brixia ran her hands over the same space. There
were cracks and crevices enough to provide her with a
means of ascent. She hesitated, her hands planted
firmly against the stone. Folly! She could still turn

back—reach the upper slopes of the dale unseen. Why was she doing this?

She had no answer save that some compulsion deep within kept her to it. Slinging her spear across her shoulder by the thong which held it during her travels, the girl put her fingers and toes to searching out a ladder way of her own.

Uta flattened her furry body on the top of the wall, peering down as if she wished to know whether Brixia followed her or not before she went on. As Brixia did start to climb, the cat, with a flirt of her tail, vanished.

Would the ruins of the manor cloak her passing over the wall from those in the copse? Brixia had no idea, she could only hope so. Listening, she could still hear the clamor of the disturbed birds, and she judged from that the skulkers were yet under cover.

On the other side of the wall stretched the paved courtyard which fronted both the fortified, and now half razed, house, and the tower at its side. Brixia dropped, having chosen to land in some rankly growing vegetation rooted below in a patch of wind gathered soil.

From that she made a dash to the shattered side of the house, moving beside it until there remained only a last crossing of the open to reach the tower door. Uta was before her, just disappearing into that opening. Brixia took a deep breath, and unslung her spear. She had no intention of entering there without her weapon to hand. It might be that she would not be judged a friend—or at least an ally.

A sprint took her to the door, she dodged inside before any sound she had made could act as warning. The dusk within was only partly dispelled by a hearth fire. Near that sat the man, watching the flames, Uta beside him. But the boy was on his feet, facing her, bared steel in hand.

Brixia hastened to speak before he could move. She wanted no struggle with him.

"There are lurkers in the wood. Your fire smoke drew them perhaps—" She waved one hand to the hearth, the spear ready held in the other. "Or you might even have been trailed here. You have a horse, there's his mail," now she gestured to the man, "those alone would be lures for any outlaw."

"What's it to you?" the boy demanded.

"Nothing. Save that I am no wolfhead." Brixia retreated a step. Her thoughts were confused. Why had she allied herself with these two who indeed meant nothing to her?

The boy watched her even as he moved in turn to stand before the man as a shield.

"You stand alone," Brixia continued, "as far as any fight is concerned. They'll lick you up as easily as Uta takes a mouse, and far more speedily, for they do not hunt for sport."

His expression of wariness did not change. "And if I do not believe you?"

She shurugged. "Have it your way then. I do not put iron at your back to urge you into battle." She glanced around the chamber in which they had taken refuge. Against the wall to her right was a steep flight of stairs leading up to the next story. This room had a bench against one wall, a stool on which the man sat, a pair of saddle bags. Two cloaks had been used on top of hacked branches and grass to form a pair of beds. That was all.

Her eyes came back to the bench. That offered a forlorn chance, but it was all they had. She did not believe that they could dare to retreat now—the boy might be able to move under cover, but burdened by the man—no—

"That," she pointed with the spear to the bench, "can go across the door—if you had not the fire you might have hidden up there," she nodded to the stair. "That's if they did not trail you in and know just how few they face."

He thrust his sword back in its scabbard and was already heading toward the bench. Brixia slung her spear and went to the other end of that. The boy looked up at her as he bent over to take a hold.

"Let be! We do not need you! I stand by Lord Marbon—"

"Do so. However, though I have no lord to fight for, I still have my own life." She caught the other end of the bench and heaved. Shuffling together they brought it to form a low barrier when placed across the doorway—a nearly useless one the girl privately thought.

"If only—" The boy glanced to the man by the fire. It appeared to Brixia that he was not speaking to her, rather voicing some thought. Then his attention returned to her and there was an open scowl on his face. He laced his fingers together, cracking his knuckles.

He spoke again—as if the words were pulled out of him by forceful extraction, and he hated the fact that he must say this:

"There might be a way out—he would know."

Brixia, remembering how she herself had long ago won out of just such a place, knew a sudden leap of hope, as quickly vanquished. If the Lord of Eggarsdale had had any emergency exit from his domain it was either destroyed in the taking of the keep, or else its

secret was so lost in the mazes of a disturbed mind that
it could never be known now.

"He will not remember." Then she added, because
any one will cling to hope, "Will he?"

The boy shrugged. "Sometimes he can a little—"
He went to kneel by his charge.

Once again Uta had raised to her hind legs, was
resting her forepaws on the man's knee. His hand
caressed her head, though he still stared into the
flames.

"Lord," the boy put out his hand, "Lord Marbon—"

Brixia took up a position by the door, dividing her
attention between what was happening in the room
and listening for any sound from without which might
mean those others were moving in. There came the
whinny of a horse—and she grew tense, bringing up
her spear.

"Lord Marbon—" the boy's voice was sharper,
more insistent. "Lord Jartar has sent a message—"

"Jartar? He is coming at last?"

"Lord, he would meet with you. He waits by the far
end of the inner ways."

"The inner ways? Why does he not come openly?"

"Lord, the enemy holds about us. He dares not try
to ride openly. Is it not always Lord Jartar's way to
come and go unseen?"

"True. The inner ways then." The man stood up,
Uta now rubbing against his legs. He surveyed the cat
and there was life and animation in his face. "Ha,
furred one. It is good to have one of your house again
allied with us, as in the days that were. The inner
ways—then."

He walked with a free stride quite unlike the aimless
shuffle, to the end of that cavern within the thick keep
wall which housed the hearth and their small fire. With

his hands he stroked the stone there even as he had stroked Uta.

His fingers, which had moved so confidently as if he knew exactly what he must do, slowed. One hand dropped to his side, he raised the other to rub along his forehead as he looked to the boy over his shoulder.

"What—" all assertive life was gone from his voice. "What—"

Uta stood up on her hind legs, her paws dangling before her lighter underbody fur. She mewed softly, authoritatively. Lord Marbon looked to her. His attitude was one of listening, he might well have understood the sounds the cat made.

"Lord," the boy moved in upon his other side. "Remember—Lord Jartar is waiting!"

The man looked about. He had not lost all the look of intelligence, though that apathy seemed to be sliding back over his face once again.

"This—this is not—not—right—" His glance took in the walls, the bareness of the chamber.

Brixia could have gnawed her fingers in her impatience. Her imagination, which seemed to have been suddenly aroused, pictured for her what might be creeping up outside. That they could hold the tower room was impossible. Also that she had allowed herself to be caught in this trap for some foolish and not understood reason aroused her anger against herself. But caught they were—even if the boy spoke the truth and this Lord Marbon had a hidden bolt hole—that such might lead from this very room was yet to be proven. Or that the cracked brain could remember—

"Jartar—yes!" Once more the use of that name appeared to pull together the man's scattered thoughts—just as the strings set on the doll by a puppet showman (such as she had seen once long ago) brought to life carved wood and leather.

Once more Lord Marbon put out his hands to the

wall. Brixia heard what she had feared from outside—a sound which could only have been the scrap of a boot against stone. She readied her spear and then looked to the stairway. Why had she not seen before the possibility of that? The two of them—with sword and spear, might have held the top of that stair—at least buying a few more moments of life. The knife in her belt—that would be *her* last key out, better than any fate she would be offered—

The sound from outside was not repeated. But she did not doubt she had heard it. Only a louder grating snapped her head around for a moment. Beside the fireplace a gap in the wall had appeared. Into that the boy pushed, suddenly and with full force, his lord. Uta sprang, vanished in the darkness, and, as the boy stepped within, giving no warning to her, Brixia sped in turn. The gap was closing but she braced the spear as a lever and fought her way in. As she pulled out the shaft again, the wall swung totally closed leaving her in deep darkness, so thick it was like a tangible cloak about her.

Brixia heard sounds from her right, and she put out her hand slowly. The space in which she stood was very small, with a wall to her left and another directly before her. With an idea of either a climb or a descent in her mind, Brixia used the spear to sound a way to the right.

Tapping before her she went some five steps until the floor vanished. Still using the spear as a guide the girl discovered there the first of what might be steps. At that point she paused to listen again. Sounds were continuing from that direction. So, if she was ever to find her way out, she must follow.

Brixia tapped her way with the spear, testing each step before she took it. Her left hand slipped along a wall which was dry at first, and then grew slimed with moisture the farther she descended. Now there was the smell of stagnant water and other foul things. Twice her hand burst a fungi growth making her cough from the acrid stench that loosed.

She counted twenty steps in that stairway then her spear cane warned her of level space ahead. The sounds made by those she trailed were muted. Brixia wondered how they could have drawn so far ahead. Unless they went without taking the precautions that she thought it prudent to exercise.

There was a complete absence of light and the dark weighing on her spirit, gave easy rise to that fear with which her species had ever regarded night and what might crawl in it. She loathed the slimy feel of the wall, but at the same time she needed to touch that as an additional guide through this place. How long these "inner ways" might run was an unknown factor. Such escape passages were usually set up so that the exit would be well beyond any besieging force. That in Moorachdale had been twice the length of the village street—or so she had always heard it said.

Now she felt a breath of air moving against her cheek. It was not strong nor fresh enough to banish the stench of slime and the unseen wall growths, but it did signify that there was some ventilation here. Brixia pushed forward, her calloused feet encountering the same moisture and slime as cloaked the wall. Once the girl was nearly shocked out of her iron control when something she trod upon wriggled. She leaped away, her feet slipping, until only a quick twist of her body kept her from falling full length into the noisome mess on the floor.

Brixia discovered a turn in the passage by running full face into the right hand wall. At her left now showed a very faint gray which was shut out twice and then revealed once again—a change which must signify the passage of the others.

The way sloped up and she drew a deeper

breath of relief, believing that she was nearing its end.
Only to know disappointment when she reached the
source of the light. For that filtered through a crack in
the rock and proved to be far too narrow to do more
than allow something as slender as her spear to penetrate. However, the very small portion of light did
show another turn, this time to the right.

Brixia was about five strides along that when there
came a burst of real light, the red-orange of flame,
ahead, and toward that she hurried. The glow showed
her that the passage she followed ended on an edge of
a ledge. She looked down into what had been a
natural cave without the sign of any tampering by
man.

Against the wall, holding a torch, was Lord Marbon.
She could see only the back of the boy who was on his
knees crawling into a hole at the other side of the cave.
Of Uta there was no sign. Although he held the torch,
Lord Marbon had lost that return of reason which had
brought them into this underground way. He stared
vacantly ahead, his eyes wide and unblinking in the
shine of the flames. But, as Brixia slipped down beside
him, ready to pass by and attempt the new passage on
her own, he turned his head slowly to look at her.

Something stirred deep in his eyes, his lips moved—

"Star blazed, grim and bright,
Darkness triumphed over right—"

The girl was startled. Then she recognized the lines
he had sung—the song of Zarsthor's Bane.

"Find it—must find it—" He spoke hurriedly, slur-
ring his words together. Marbon caught at her arm,
showing surprising strength, for he held her quiet so,
and she knew that, short of using force, she could not
break free. "Nothing's right—it is because of
Zarsthor's Bane." He lowered his head a little, thrust-

ing his face closer to hers. "Must find—" The recognition of a sort made his eyes fully alive.

"Not—Jartar! Who are you?" His voice was sharp, held a ring of command.

"I am Brixia," she returned, wondering just how much his wandering sense had returned.

"Where is Jartar? Did he send you then?" His grip on her was tight and steady enough so that when he shook her, her whole body moved.

"I do not know where Jartar is," she tried to find some words which would satisfy this lord who, by the evidence of the boy, called on a dead man. "Perhaps—" she used the same excuse his attendant had, "he is waiting outside."

Lord Marbon considered that. "He knows, from the ancient runes—only he— I must have it! He promised that it was mine to use. I am the last of Zarsthor's line. I must have it!" He shook her again as if he would force what he wanted out of her by such rough mishandling. Now her hand closed about the hilt of her belt knife. If it were necessary to use that for protection against a mad man—why, then she would.

But it was not only his visible madness which aroused her fears—it was something inside herself. Her head—she wanted to cry out—to wrench free of this Marbon and run and run— Because—deep in her she stood in front of a door and if that door would open—!

This was not the shrinking that the sane sometimes feel when confronted by the abnormal among their own species. Her new emotion was totally alien. She could not turn her head, break the tie between their eyes. There was a need rising in her—something she must do—and nothing else in all the world mattered but that need which compelled, which made her its prisoner. She found herself whispering:

"Zarsthor's Bane." That was it! What she must

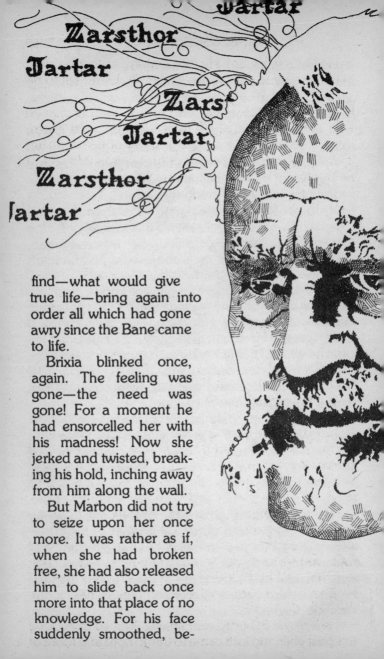

Zarsthor
Jartar
Jartar
Zars
Jartar
Zarsthor
Jartar

find—what would give true life—bring again into order all which had gone awry since the Bane came to life.

Brixia blinked once, again. The feeling was gone—the need was gone! For a moment he had ensorcelled her with his madness! Now she jerked and twisted, breaking his hold, inching away from him along the wall.

But Marbon did not try to seize upon her once more. It was rather as if, when she had broken free, she had also released him to slide back once more into that place of no knowledge. For his face suddenly smoothed, became entirely vacant. He stared at the wall, not at her. While the hand with which he had held her fell to his side.

The hole which might lead to the open beckoned her, but Brixia was afraid to go to hands and knees, leaving her back unprotected, lest he pounce upon her again. So they stood against opposite sides of the cave as she tried to determine a way of quick escape.

"Lord—" the boy's head suddenly appeared in the hole, "all is clear without."

Brixia burst forth, eager to share her knowledge of what might be a danger.

"Your lord is crazed."

The boy's face contracted with rage as he scrambled to his feet.

"You lie! He took a bad hurt at the Pass of Ungo— the same time as his foster brother was slain. His hurt and his sorrow has upset for a time his knowledge of what we do and where we go. He is *not* crazed!"

His lips twisted into a snarl. Brixia thought that inwardly he must agree with her, but some emotion would not let him admit it.

"He is back here—in his home," the boy continued. "The healer said that were he in a place he knew well, his memory could return to him. He—he thinks he is on a quest. It is an old tale of his House—the story of Zarsthor's Bane. He would gain the Bane and put all right again. It is that belief which has kept him alive.

"It is an old legend of his line—of how Zarsthor who came to Eggarsdale crossed the brother of his lady— she was of the Old Ones—and Eldor in his pride and rage made a pact with some dark power, laying upon Zarsthor and his blood after him, even onto the land he then held, a curse so that when they gained aught, they lost the more.

"When the fighting went against him so grievously this past year, my lord came to think more and more of the Bane. And Lord Jartar, who had ever an interest in ancient stories, more so if they dealt with the Old Ones, spoke with him often. So it became fixed in my lord's mind there was perhaps after all a true meaning in this story out of the past. Thus my lord made a pact with the Lord Jartar—who swore that he had chanced upon some secrets which might lead to the unraveling of this story of the Bane—that they would indeed search out the truth of Zarsthor and what might lie hidden in the past—"

"But how does one find secrets out of the past?" In spite of herself Brixia was caught by a faint excitement. For the first time in a long march of days she was drawn to an idea which was not strictly a part of her fight to keep on living from one day's dawn to sunset, from sunset to the next dawn.

The boy shrugged, his face held a bitter twist of mouth, a frowning pull of eyebrow toward eyebrow.

"Ask that of the Lord Jartar—or rather of his shade! He is dead, but the Bane lives in my lord's mind. And maybe it possesses him now past the point whereby he can believe in aught else!"

Brixia bit her lip. The boy had already turned away from her. Perhaps Marbon had ensorcelled him, too after the fashion which had worked on her for those few moments when they were alone here. It could well be that in truth it was the lord's delusion which had led them both to this ruined valley, rather than any advice from a healer.

She watched the boy take the torch from his companion, lead the man to the hole and gently force him to hands and knees, then push him towards that exit. Once set in motion Lord Marbon did not resist, but crawled on into the dark. When he had vanished the boy thrust the torch into a crack in the rock and dropped to follow.

Brixia, having no mind to remain underground if

there was a way out, crept in herself, on the other's heels.

The narrow passage was a short one, and they came out into a deeper twilight where several trees and some brush formed a curtain before the break in the ground through which they had come. They were well up on the northern slope of the dale's guarding hills. As they squatted there, under the cover of the brush, Brixia surveyed the keep below. Faint light played in one of the tower's slit windows—there must still be fire within. Also she was able to count five shaggy, ill-kempt ponies, the like of which outlaws rode, if they were lucky enough to be mounted at all.

"Five—" she heard the boy half whisper beside her. He, too, had wriggled forward until his shoulder nudged against hers.

"Perhaps more," she told him with some satisfaction. "Some bands number more men than mounts."

"We shall have to take to the hills again," he commented bleakly. "That or into the Waste."

In spite of herself Brixia felt something of his discouragement. She was resentful of having to think of anyone but herself, but if these two wandered on without any supplies, or any more knowledge of woodcraft than she guessed they had, they might already be counted dead men. It irked her that she was not allowed by that strange nagging, new born within her, to leave them to the fate they courted by their folly.

"Has your lord no kin to shelter him?" she asked.

"None. He—he was not always accepted among those soft-handed, lower dales people. He—has, as I said, other blood—from *THEM*—" Among the Dalesmen "them" so accented meant only one thing—those alien peoples who had once held all this land. "He—that was what made him what he was—what he is. You wouldn't understand—you've only seen him now," the boy's voice was a passionate whisper, as if he feared he might not be able to keep his self control. "He was a great warrior—and he was learned, too. He knew things other Dale lords never dreamed of understanding. He could call birds to him and talk to them—I have seen him do that! And there wasn't a horse what wouldn't come and let him ride. He could sing a sleep spell for a wounded man. I have even seen him lay hands on a wound which was black with poison and order the flesh to heal—it did! But there was no one who could so heal him, no one!"

The boy's head sunk forward until his face was hidden in the crook of his arm. He lay quietly but Brixia stirred as there spread from him into her an almost overpowering sense of pain and loss.

"You were his squire?"

"After Jartar died I carried his shield, yes. But I was not rightfully a squire. Though I might have been some day if all had gone well. My Lord took me by choice from among his mother's distant kin. I—had no great possessions to hope for—we held but a border watch tower and there were two more brothers—so there was no favor right for me. It's all gone now anyway— all but my lord—all but my lord!"

His voice was thick, and he hunched his shoulder in her direction. Brixia knew that he hated her knowing these feelings. She must let him alone and ask no more.

Turning, she edged away from that vantage point. But—where they had left Lord Marbon—there was no one! She looked around quickly—there was no sign of him—

4

"HE'S GONE!"

Her cry brought the boy shoving past her. Then he was on his feet, completely unheeding of any other eyes which might be watching from below. Brixia tried to catch at him, remind him of their present peril. But her move came too late, he had plunged into the brush on the other side of that pocket-sized clearing. Plainly nothing mattered but his Lord as far as he was concerned.

Brixia remained where she was. Now that they were safe out of that keep trap, there was no need for her to company longer with the two of them. No need at all. Only, no matter how much her prudence insisted upon that, still she was, a moment or so later, moving reluctantly to follow the boy.

Of Uta there was no sign either. Perhaps the cat, for some purpose of her own, had gone with Lord Marbon. Slowly Brixia pushed through the bushes in the same direction the boy had taken.

Chance continued to favor them with cover, for beyond the bushes there was a sunken trough in the ground, much overgrown with vines and brush. Newly broken twigs and torn leaves marked that as the path. Brixia advanced along the cut warily. Though there was little danger of being surprised by any wild thing large or vicious enough to attack without warning, there might well be other things loose in this dank place—things suited to nest among such growth.

For there was much about these bushes, the vines, which was forbidding. Fleshy leaves were a dark

53

green, so dark as to appear smoked into blackness. Some were veined with red or a rusty yellow-brown— like dried blood. From those which had been crushed by passing of those she trailed there arose a musky

odor, unpleasant, different from any vegetation she had smelled before.

The branches and stems were black, and that blackness, touching against Brixia's arms, her body,

left streakings upon her flesh and clothing as if they exuded moisture. She used the spear as best she could to push low hanging limbs out of her way.

Now the girl suspected that this path, cut between two ever rising banks, could not be natural. Had it been fashioned by some now dried stream it would have run from the north—down slope. But this angled east to west along the side of the ridge. It must have been made to hide those emerging from the bolt hole, guide them towards the Waste.

Twice Brixia halted, determined to turn back, or at least scramble up out of this ill-omened path. Yet each time she surveyed the growth along its walls doubtfully (the brush obviously thicker there) she shrank from forcing an opening through it.

During her last halt she heard enough to bring her spear to ready. No voice had been raised in a true whisper, no crashing sounded from ahead or behind. She stood, seemingly isolated, in a dull, dark green walled tunnel utterly alone.

No—that did not issue from small gust of wind lifting the thick puffy leaves, nor—

The girl faced toward the way she had come, striving to identify the sound. It was a—a chittering—a clicking, as if teeth struck upper jaw against the lower. She had heard once or twice a noise not too unlike it when Uta had watched a bird beyond her reach.

"Uta!" Brixia called softly—at the same time knowing deep in her mind that this was not the cat. The sound was spaced—it might form words of so alien a tongue that she had no hope of translation.

From behind? No, as she listened, tense, she was sure that sound did not echo up the tunnel which had grown deeper until the brush along its walls met to form a roof over her head. It—she stared downward—and a cold fear grew in her—it was as if that came from underground!

Every instinct urged her to go crashing ahead in instant flight. But—perhaps that was what was wanted of her. Instead, making an effort for control, she paused, her head a little on one side, listening to that clicking. Then she saw—the way ahead only a fraction visible under the combination of dusk and the over-shadowed path, was shifting! Under the thick layer of leaves which made a rot-muck into which her feet sank there was a—sinking! The ground itself—yes, she could feel a change in it! She had a sudden and horrifying vision of the path falling down, away, into some gulf, taking her with it. And that in the hidden burrow under her feet there awaited—

She dared no longer hesitate here! Fearfully Brixia kept eyeing the ground under that mat of leaves reduced to slime which bespatted her bare feet with every step she took. What if some—some *thing* would now rear up to make sure of her capture?

The girl broke and ran. With a rising of the walls, or the sinking of the path, the way was clearer. She did not have to fight so hard to get through. By straining for sight she could see the tracks in the mould. The others—or one of them—was still ahead. Now she wanted nothing more than to be in the company of her own kind.

She hated and feared the blur of shadows. While the stench of both the broken leaves and the muck stirred up underfoot was sickening. Brixia hurried on, aware now that the path under her feet was now steady and rising, as if aiming to cross over the ridge height. Twice she slipped as that climbing angle steepened. Here there were marks in plenty to show that the others had fallen or been forced to scramble ahead with increasing difficulty.

Slightly ahead, was a tangle of broken branches, crushed leaves, some twigs still quivering. Thrusting through at the same spot she came out in the open under a lowering sky. Yet there was enough light left to hearten her a little. Before her a ledge jutted into open space. On three sides that looked to be without any escape and for a dazed moment or so she wondered if the boy and Lord Marbon had somehow fallen off this exposed perch. Having very little head for heights, Brixia (there being none to witness her lapse from confidence) drew near the left hand side of the ledge on hands and knees, even then quailing before looking down.

What she saw was astounding. There was no mistaking here the hand of man—or else that of some intelligent being who had altered nature to serve its purpose. For below, hugging what was otherwise a steep cliff, descended a flight of stairs. Weather worn, covered with lichen, those steps angled steeply down to the floor of a narrow valley. While on the cliff which side-flanked these were hollows and ridges of

carving—also weather worn and mottled by lichen.

Dusk deepened fast. In the limited light those lines and depressions seemed to leer or scowl, forming faces so alien that Brixia quickly turned her eyes away from the wall. Below she heard a rattle of falling stone and saw movement. There was a curious hazy cover for the ground below—quite a distance below as if the base of this narrow valley was far under her perch, much deeper than that on the side of the ridge from which she had come.

There the shadows lay very thick. But these were not yet dark enough to mask the two who stood by an outcrop of stone. Even as her gaze centered on them, the larger broke from the grasp of the smaller. Brushing aside his companion when the other tried to stop him, the taller kept on westward, striding with the measured step used by the practiced traveler.

Determined to catch up, Brixia arose, fighting the feeling of being about to pitch forward from heights, and began to descend the stairway. One hand went out to find holds in the carvings, for the wide open space to her right made her head swim. Deliberately she schooled herself to look only at what lay immediately before her.

By the time she reached the end of that way, for she had dared not hurry, the other two were again well ahead. This second valley being strangely bare of any vegetation, she could see them in spite of an odd wavering of outline.

Brixia rubbed her eyes, thinking that perhaps it was her own sight which caused that difficulty in seeing more distant objects. For whole moments the way was clear, then again, when she looked down at her own feet or at one of the outcrops of stone (and those were many) all was a blur.

At least the air here was clear and she could breathe without drawing into her lungs the stifling stench cling-

ing to that upper path. Here, though, the footing was
hard for her unshod feet, drifts of gravel and small
stones tormented even her well toughened soles. At
last Brixia was reduced to a slow pace, lest she render
herself too foot sore to move. She regretted those
sandals lying back in her pack—abandoned in the
dale. Several times she was tempted to raise her voice
in a shout to those ahead, begging them to wait for her.
With the dark so close upon them surely sooner or
later they too would be driven to halt.

The girl had seen nothing of the cat since she had
entered that passage in the keep, and Brixia wondered
now if Uta had indeed come down from the upper
ridge at all. Somehow it was important that Uta be one
with them. She found herself worrying lest Uta had
gone off on her own.

The dusk thickened, and, with that deepening of the
dark, the girl became more and more wary. Perhaps
that strange, invisible, chitterer of the covered way did
not follow here, but the sense that she was not alone,
that there was that which spied upon her, gripped
tighter with each hobbling step which she forced herself to take.

To halt here was more than she could do. She
wanted company—any company—to banish that feeling of being utterly at the mercy of some unknown.
Now and again she paused for the space of a breath or
two, listening—to discover that in this valley were
none of the reassuring noises which filled nights in the
open. No insect chirruped or buzzed, no bird called—
the silence was complete, so that her own breathing
sounded loud in her ears, an accidental scrape of her
spear haft against the stone as sharp as the war horn of
a keep company.

There was—Brixia tried to subdue her imagination.
It was *not* true that she walked amid a throng of
unseen things! Nothing moved save herself. Shaking

with more than the chill of the night Brixia steadied her body against a stone which stood shoulder high beside her.

Her fingers moved over a pit, a ridge—She turned her head to look. A face—!

What sorcery made the crude carving stand out against the stone, visible through the dark, she could not guess. It was as if her touch had awakened inanimate stone into a spark of life.

A face—? No, there was nothing remotely human in the features of that mask. The eyes were huge, round, and each was centered with a small spark of flame which formed a pinpoint of greenish white light. Where nose and mouth should have appeared there was rather sketched, in a diabolically realistic form of art, a wide muzzle-mouth a little agape, enough to show the tips of sharply pointed fangs.

For the rest—Brixia made herself look, refusing to be cowed—once she had gotten over her first astonishment—it was really but lines on stone—there was nothing more—just that mouth and the eyes. Perhaps the ones who had wrought that expected the viewers' imagination to build the rest in their minds alone. Shame at being shaken by such a trick thing, Brixia struck the stone with her spear and then hurried on, in spite of the pain of her feet. She refused to look over her shoulder as she went, though she was troubled by a feeling that there was something in sly pursuit.

There was no doubt in her mind, that she now was traversing a place of the Old Ones. And, Brixia thought, of a species who were not inclined to favor any human encroachment on their territory. This was not, as that place Kuniggod had taken her to, a refuge. Rather it posed an abiding threat to those of her kind.

The narrow cut of the valley, as much as she could see of it in the dark, widened out into a much larger area. Once more the girl hesitated. To wander on into the night with no guide was perhaps folly. If those she sought followed a trail, she had seen no sign of such since she had descended the cliff stairway. But at least here the foot punishing gravel had given away to patches of grass.

Moving from one of those to the next she could not keep a straight line, but did save her feet from further torment. While ahead—Would those other two be foolish enough to light a fire again? Here in the open that could only center on them the attention of any prowlers abroad in the night.

The Waste had always had an evil name, and there were rumors of all kinds of non-human life which were to be encountered here. Its sinister barrenness formed a western border to the Dales which supported, of her own kind, only the outlaws and a few strange men who were attracted by remnants of what they thought they had discovered concerning the Old Ones. It was to the Waste that the lords of the Dales had, in their extremity of the seasons just past, gone for help against the invaders. And from the Waste had come that help—the wereriders—whom all men knew were not men at all but a daunting combination of man and feral beast. That story had spread even to the few contacts Brixia had dared to make, landmen in hiding, as surly and suspicious as she herself had become but sometimes willing to exchange a handful of salt for a brace of leaper skins.

She had in her drifting, her fleeing and hiding, during the past two years skirted the Waste many times. Mainly because human enemies continued to lurk between her and what refuges might still exist farther east. She had watched the swarming of outlaws to and from its borders. But she had never ventured out into its depths.

That the Lord Marbon with his disordered wits

might do this—that could be expected. But that she need follow him— Brixia dropped to crouch on one of the patches of grass, rubbing at her feet, her eyes wide, her ears alert as she looked and listened— The dark hid most of what was to be seen, but there were sounds out of the night here, not that frightening silence which had held the valley.

While—she held her head high— Into her nostrils Brixia drew air scented with a fragrance which could be at the other end of a balance from the rotting stench of the narrow upper path. Sweet, fresh—she thought of meadow grass lying in the early morning, webs on it pearled with dew—flowers just opening to the day. There was a garden—open to the sun of mid-morning—its blossoms ready to be harvested and dried for the sweetening of bed clothes and body linen— It was—

Without being quite aware of what she did Brixia got once more to her feet—moved on into the night, drawn by that scent which grew ever the stronger. So she came to the foot of a tree— Oddly twisted were its branches, and those lacked leaves. But it was aflower and the flowers were white. Seeming to extend from the tip of each petal—like the glow of a small candle—was a wisp of light.

Brixia put out her hand, but did not quite dare to touch petal or branch. She was standing in awe and wonder when a hoarse croak aroused her.

The girl faced about, her spear at ready. Faint as was the light diffused by the flowers she caught a glimpse of what lurked there. Though they were little, the noise they made when they saw her mindful of them was loud as something twice their size could have raised. Small, yes, but in them lay horror.

If a toad might rise upon its hind legs, show evil intelligence in its bulbous eyes, fangs within its gaping mouth—then that might approach in appearance

these croaking things. Save that these toad creatures had no smooth skin—rather that was covered with ragged patches of very coarse hair—hair—or fine tendrils. A longer growth weaved from each corner of their mouths, matching similar ones set one above each eye. These were in constant motion as if the unwholesome threads had a separate life of their own.

Brixia set her back against the tree trunk. They did not move in upon her as she had expected them to do. That their purpose was utterly evil she had no doubt at all. For there beat into her mind a cold hatred of all she was and they were not. Instead of an open attack, they began to circle to the right, moving one after another at a lurching gait—a ghastly parody of one of the round dances mankind indulged in at feast times.

They were silent now, but as each passed her, knowing eyes were turned in her direction, and in each she read the foulness of their desires. Round, they must be making a circle of the tree. Brixia herself slipped around its bole, keeping that ever within touching distance of her shoulders, striving to see if she were entirely ringed about.

What they desired, the girl could not guess. But she knew well there was a purpose to this capering. Faint memories of some of Kuniggod's stories came to her. There was a way of working magic by the repetition of ritual words, or in the performance of certain acts in a set pattern. Was that what was happening here and now?

If so—she must break their pattern before their magic was complete. How to do that—?

Holding her spear ready, Brixia dashed from the tree towards the nearest portion of the circle. The things gave before her, but they merely drew back a fraction, to continue their circling just beyond the reach of her spear. While from them came a feeling of malicious amusement. She was sure they did not fear her, that they intended to prance so until their purpose was achieved.

If she was to break through that circle, over leap them, or use her spear to hinder them long enough to be free—would she truly be free at all? To venture away from even the meagre light given forth by the tree flowers was to be caught dark-blind in their own territory where they could hunt her down with ease.

Brixia backed once more under the branches and the upstanding blossom lights. She was sure that the circle narrowed slightly with each revolution that the dancers made. Soon she would have to make up her mind firmly and keep to it. Either break free or suffer whatever they wished to happen. Such indecision was not usually hers but neither was she accustomed to facing an enemy so far removed from all she knew.

Under the tree there was a sensation of safety. Which might be only a suggestion born from her need and hope. Brixia touched the back of the trunk, gave a start. She might then have fingered warmth of flesh. In that instant of contact there had sped a message into her mind. Had that *really* happened? Or again was she bemused and misled—perhaps by the same magic the creatures evoked?

There was one way of making sure of that. Setting her spear in the crook of her arm Brixia gently pulled down a branch only a little above her head. Again, out of nearly forgotten years, she recalled something of those words Kuniggod had always used when she went harvesting among the garden plants. What she said to each shrub, bush or smaller green things, before she culled its blossoms. For Kuniggod had firmly believed that growing life had a spirit also which should be recognized and appeased by any gleaner.

"For my use spare me of your bounty, green sister. Rich is your store, the fruit of your body. Beauty is yours and sweetness—and that which you freely give, that alone shall I take."

The girl placed her hand above a flower. The light its petals shed erased the wind and sun browning of her flesh, instead gave the soft lustre of a water gem to pearl her fingers. She did not need to exert any strength to free the blossom from its parent stem. No, it was as if it loosed itself, to settle gently in her grasp.

For a long moment she hesitated, even forgetting the dance of the toad things, expecting that, once free of its branch , the wonder she held upon the flattened palm of her hand would fade, lose its gentle radiance. But it did not, and there grew in her such a sense of peace, of rightness with the world as she had not remembered since that morning she had awakened in the place of the Old Ones.

Once more she spoke to the tree—or maybe not to a tree but an entity she could not see, could not touch with any sense, save that stir within her.

"My thanks to you, green sister. Your free gift is my treasure."

Moving, not by any conscious will, but as one who is asleep, and, within a dream acts out some deep hidden desire, Brixia let fall the spear, leaving herself defenseless by the standards of her kind.

Flower in hand she walked from the shelter of the tree toward that circle which had narrowed to a point just beyond where the outmost branches overhung the ground. Towards the whirling figures, whose dance had grown even faster, she went confidently, grasping the blossom. A cloud of fragrance moved with her.

There was a croaking screech and the toad immediately before her stopped short. Its mouth stretched as it uttered hoarse gibbering sounds which might have been speech but none known to mankind. Brixia stretched out her hand. The flower's light streamed between her fingers.

The toad thing cowered away, crying out in anger. For a moment only it faced her defiantly. Then it turned to pelt away, still gibbering, into the dark. Those who had flanked it in the dance broke line also. They did not beat such a quick retreat, rather snarled and gabbled at her, moving their paw hands in awkward gestures. Though those paws held no weapons it was plain they threatened.

Between them and the girl the flower held its constant light, not bright, but not dimming either. The creatures edged backwards. Brixia made no move to follow them beyond the line their dance had set—the limit of the tree's overhanging branching. She knew, though not how, that the canopy of that growth represented a barrier of a sort, and for her a refuge.

There was an attempt to begin the dance once again. But, though those a little beyond her croaked and gestured, none would pass where she stood flower in hand. At last they broke in earnest, pattering off into the dark. Though they did not altogether desert the battlefield, for, as she returned to settle under the tree she could hear croaking calls, gibbering, arising through the darkness, and guessed that she now lay besieged.

She was hungry and she was thirsty. Another brief thought of the pack she had left in the dale at the beginning of this adventure made her sigh at her folly. But both hunger and thirst were muted—they might have tormented another part of her, detached from the person who sat under the tree, nursing the bloom, its petals as fine and firm as if carved of some treasured gem stone.

On impulse Brixia breathed more deeply of that fragrance. Nor was she fully conscious of what she did then as she turned to the tree behind her shoulder. Placing the flower carefully on the ground, she knelt and embraced the trunk with her arms, setting her mouth to its smooth bark. Her tongue touched that bark, swept back and forth across its surface. Though her flesh did not have the rasping abilities of Uta's, it would seem that she did so fret the wood. For there was moisture now rising to her licking. Drops oozed out which she could suck.

Neither sweet nor sour, having a taste she could not honestly give any name to, that moisture dribbled, flowing faster as her tongue continued to lick the bark, answering the sucking of her lips. She swallowed sucked, swallowed.

Thirst was gone, and hunger. Brixia was filled, revived. A murmuring enveloped her, blotting out the calls of the toad folk. Brixia lifted her head, laughed joyfully.

"Green mother you truly are! For your strength do I give thanks, Lady of the flowers! Ahhh—but what thanks can such as I render unto you?"

There was a sadness born in her. This was the emotion someone might know if she looked through a doorway into a place of great joy and yet dared not enter therein. If this was magic (and how could it be else than that?) let no man hereafter decry such magic in her hearing. The girl leaned once more against the tree and set her lips to the bark, not now for filling and comforting, but in wonder and joy.

Then she turned and curled up, the flower beside her face, her spear lying forgotten. With perfect faith in her safety she slept.

5

B<small>RIXIA</small> <small>AWOKE</small> softly and happily. The sun had arisen far enough to send gold fingers into the Waste. She lay looking up drowsily, wrapped in a strange content, into the meeting of branches over her.

Those flowers which had been candles in the night were now tight closed in sheathing of red-brown outer casing. None had faded, fallen from the branches. As she turned her head a little the girl saw the one she had plucked resting on the ground beside her, no longer wide open, but changed into a cylinder of brown as were its sisters on the tree.

She was not hungry, nor did her feet ache now. Instead she felt alert, strong. And—

Brixia shook her head. Did dreams hold over into waking hours? She could blink, close her eyes, and see, somehow with her mind, a pathway. There was growing in her a sense of compulsion, a restless feeling that she was needed somewhere—for a task she did not yet understand.

She picked up the tightly encased flower, putting it

71

into the front of her shirt where it might ride safe against her skin. Once more on her feet the girl looked to the tree and spoke softly:

"Green mother, what magic you have worked for me I am not wise enough to understand. But I do not doubt that it will smooth my path. In your name from this time forth shall I go not unmindful of all which grows from roots, lifts stems or branches to the sky. We share life truly—this lesson have I learned."

That was so. Never again would she look upon forms of life different from her own without heeding their wonder. Did one who was blind and suddenly gain sight view the world with such sharp clarity as was hers in this early morning?

Each twist of coarse grass, rise of stunted and twisted bush in the land beyond, was transformed for her into a thing rare and strange. All stood differently from its fellow, offered an infinite variety of shape.

Brixia picked up the spear. As the world of green growth had come to a new life for her, so had there also been set in her mind the way she must go. In that going she must no longer tarry. There was a need for her.

On she sped at a steady trot. Those toad things that had striven to use their sorcery to her defeat were gone. Without being told the girl knew that sunlight raised a barrier against them.

Now and then, on some patch of earth, she saw tracks; boots had pressed here. Woven in and out among those markings were the pad prints left by Uta. The three she followed had come this way.

In one place Uta's tracks were to one side, a number together. Brixia nodded, though there was no other there to see her acknowledgment of what the cat had done. Uta, she was very sure, had deliberately set those signs for her, Brixia—in a way as clear as any road sign of the Dales.

The girl no longer questioned the purpose of her own actions. Dimly she understood that she could not turn aside now from this trail.

There was life in the Waste—but none which this morning appeared threatening. Leapers jumped once or twice before her, streaking away with speed in those great bounds which had given them their country name. Brixia sighted an armor clothed lizard, its reddish scales matching the sand about the rock on which it sat. Jeweled eyes surveyed her as she passed. It did not share the leapers' fear.

A flock of birds called and fluttered up from the earth, to fly only a short distance and then light again, searching for insects. They were dun in color, as was much of this land, for there were no sharp and brilliant greens, no flowers to star the grass. The vegetation was as dusty as the soil. One or two plants with fleshy, grey-red leaves stood isolated. Around the roots of those lay shellcases of beetles, horny legs, debris of feasts dropped from the stems ending in thorned leaf pairs ready to close on new prey.

This part of the Waste did not lie level, rather possessed a number of rounded hills—like dunes of shore sand—save that these were of earth, not so easily wind-shifted. Thus the trail Brixia now followed did not run straight, but wove a way back and forth among those. As they rose higher the less far she could see.

The feeling of rightness with the world which had been hers upon awakening under the shelter of the tree had ebbed little by little as Brixia penetrated further into the maze of the mound country. Coarse grass grew on the sides of those—but the clumps did not resemble true vegetation, rather they appeared more like rank fur covering the bodies of crouching beasts who allowed her to venture in so far amidst their herd so she would prove easy prey when they ceased to toy cruelly with her and sprang—

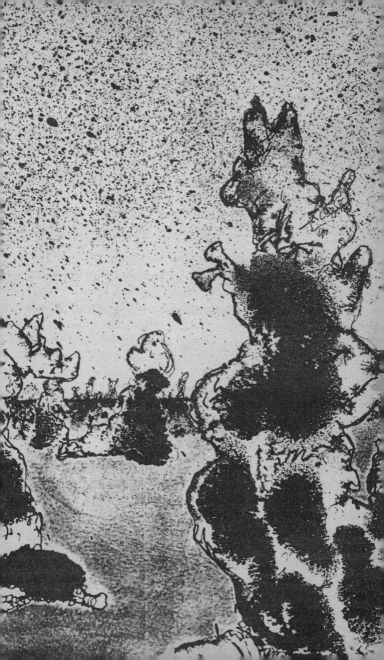

Fancies—yes, but such as were not normally like her to dwell upon. Brixia even paused twice to thud her spear point into a mound side just because she must so reassure herself that this was indeed only dank earth and grass and no such menace as creeping thought suggested.

A portion of her mind arose to question. These fear-forms—surely they were not hers. Fear she had long known, but that was all of tangible things, wolves of her own breed, cold, hunger, sickness—all which was ready to assault the helpless or the careless. Never had she drawn upon fancy to supply new enemies.

Brixia wanted to run blindly, in any direction which would take her free of this weaving way. Better a parched, dry desert than this! But she fought hard against these fancies; instead of taking flight as her pounding heart urged, she deliberately slowed her pace, set herself to concentrate upon one thing alone—the watching for those signs of a trail which the others had left her.

It was only then when she concentrated fully on that Brixia discovered that, while here and there was a boot mark plainly to read, a more important sign was missing. Here Uta had left no paw print.

Brixia came to a sharp halt. The lack of those paw prints rang a stout warning signal in her mind. She did not understand why it was so necessary that she be sure she followed where the cat led, but it was— enough to send her facing around.

She did not like the idea of retracing the way she had come. Nor, she argued with herself, might it be needful. But—her hand sought without thinking the furled flower bud pressed against her breast, safe so within her clothing— But—she was as certain as if a command which must be obeyed had rung out of the air over her head—this she *must* do.

Even more did the mounds take on unlikely, eerie

shapes. Brixia felt that they were solid earth only when she faced them squarely, fighting down her fear. From eye corner they seemed to swell, to diminish, to take on strange outlines—

She broke into a trot, one hand still pressing the flower tightly above her heart, the other holding the spear at ready. Then—

There was a mound directly before her, as if it had arisen full humped out of the ground to box her in. The marks her own feet had left ran on—and vanished against the rise of the mound. This could not be—was it illusion? Some of Kuniggod's half remembered tales flitted back from far memory. Brixia raised the spear and, without truly thinking of what she did, hurled it with full force of arm.

The point sank into soil, the shaft quivered a little. That was no illusion! Solid earth did block her retreat. She had been sucked into some kind of trap, the bait those tracks. Brixia put out her hand and retrieved her spear.

She must *not* panic. Though she was shaking a little, her hand so damp as it closed about the haft of her weapon that the wood turned a fraction in her grasp. She hated to turn her back on that mound which should not have been there. But she had to make a choice. To linger where she was would solve nothing at all. That courage, which she had learned as a matter of self preservation, argued that, now warned, she could do no better than go on and face what she must face—better sooner than later when fear had longer to gnaw at her resolution.

Once more she strode along the trail she had followed earlier. The boot marks were easy to read. Where had those three really gone? How long since she had been enticed from the real trail? It was useless to raise such questions now. She had no one to depend upon but herself.

But whoever had arranged that trap seemed in no hurry to announce its, or their, presence. She found that wearing, too. To be ever ready for an attack which did not come took the fine edge from her preparedness even as the edge could be blunted on a blade.

Around one mound and then another and then—

It was like stepping from a curtain darkened room into the full light of day. Earlier she had wished for desert, to be rid of the shadow throwing mounds. Now Brixia found her wish answered, but she liked the prospect far less than she believed she would.

Before her stretched open country, bare of even the tattered bushes and clumps of grass which had marked that lying on the edge of the Waste. Here was only yellow, red streaked, earth, worn by a network of channels which ran in so many opposing directions Brixia could not believe they had ever been cut by the water of some past flood.

Outcrops of stone, of a sullen red with thick veins of black, raised like protesting fists towards the sky in which hung a sun that gave a blazing heat to meet Brixia like a wave from the open door of a keep bread oven.

She gasped. To go into that, set her bare feet on that parched and furance-hot soil—such an act was impossible. Much as she distrusted the mound maze, she must return to that. Turn she did—

But where was that gap through which she had just come?

Brixia swayed, clung to the spear, set butt against the earth, as her support. She shook her head, shut her eyes, held them so closed for a long moment and then opened them once again.

What she saw *must* this time be truly illusion! Great weights of earth could not shift in the space of a few breaths to close the path down which she had come. Yet now, though she turned her head to look right and then left, there was nothing but a towering earthen wall, no break in its length.

Brixia flung herself at that rise which should have been a gap. She dug the spear point into the earth with one hand, with the other she grasped at a handful of the grass to pull herself up. If there was no longer any way through, then her answer was to climb up and over.

The edges of the grass were as sharp as the blade on which she had set a new edge—was it only a day ago? She gasped, and brought her fingers to her mouth, licking the blood which appeared in bright lines to drabble down her palm and wrist. And she jerked away lest her feet also have such cruel cuts.

Hunkering down where the dank earth of the mound's foot met the bare earth, she tried to think sensibly. That something had happened which was not of human logic, there was no doubt. That it was a threat, that she must accept also. In a way totally alien to all she had ever known, Brixia had been herded, by drifts of the earth itself, to this place.

Bleakly she understood that there was no retreat. She might be able to walk along the foot of the mound wall either north or south, but there was a growing doubt that she would be allowed to so postpone whatever fate had harried her this far. This had taken on all the evil sensation of a dream out of the always to be feared *DARK*.

That she would remain where she was and tamely await disaster—no, she summoned her determination with that encouragement she had used many times before.

"I live," she told the empty desert before her fiercely. "I have arms, legs, a body—I have a mind— I am me, Brixia! And I serve no will save my own!"

There came no answer to her defiance—unless the far off, harsh cry of what might have been some hunting bird provided that. She licked her dry lips. It seemed a very long time since she had drunk of the tree's bounty. And there was no chance of water in that red and yellow land.

But into it she would go—by her own will and choice of time—not that of the intelligence which had set her to this trail. Now she pulled off her skin jacket and set to work with her knife to cut apart those strips she had so laboriously laced together. The resulting pile of skin bits she began to fashion into foot coverings, shredding the hides into lengths which could be wrapped about her feet ankle high, and secured there with the tightest knotted thongs she could improvise.

Having finished the only protection she could manage, the girl arose to her feet, and, shading her eyes against the sun's glare with her hand, looked on across the riven land. The many sharp edged gullies formed such a network that to steer a straight course would be impossible. There were those outcrops of rock and the possibility of some shade from such. But a haze held the distance well curtained and she could not be sure what might rise, or fall, ahead.

Brixia shrugged. To wait would gain her nothing. She judged that it was well after nooning, she could hope that twilight might come with a measure of coolness. With the spear ready to use as a staff if she might have need of its support, Brixia started out into the desert.

There was enough difference in the outline of one outcrop from another that she could pick a guide ahead and so make sure she did not wander in circles. Here was one in a rounded pinnacle as if a single stumpy thumb pointed skyward. She chose that as her first objective.

Twice she had to detour because of a gully too broad for her to jump. It was like making a journey where one took three steps forward and two back. Though there were patches of bare earth here, and such were marked with tracks, none of the boot prints appeared.

The clearest of such tracks was a print with four toes, each as long as her own foot. It could be the sign of a bird—but one with such a foot—it must then stand as tall as she, even larger!

However where there were signs of life, then there must also be the means for maintaining that life. Brixia knew of no living creature which might exist without water—therefore this land could not be as dead as it looked. She stooped and chose a small red ball of a pebble and set it in her mouth, using the craft of a wanderer to serve her need.

Beside the thumb pillar she paused in the small patch of shade that provided to choose ahead another goal.

It was then that the silence of this burning waste was shattered by a scream from the air overhead. Brixia pushed back until her shoulders scraped against the sun heated rock of the outcrop. She looked up—

Across the sky wheeled a bird, not close enough yet for her to distinguish through the haze of the heat whether it was some oversize hawk such as she had

often witnessed at the hunt among the hills, or a carrion eater whose domain this was.

The scream was answered. Another one of its kind planed into view. Together they circled the thumb rock and Brixia was certain that she was their quarry. As they dropped lower she gasped.

Even the gold eagle that ruled majestically in the heights of High Hallack would be as a grass warbler compared to these. If they alighted she was certain their heads with those threatening beaks agape as they now shrieked might be on a level with her shoulders.

She held her stance against the rock which at least would protect her back if she had to defend herself from an out and out attack, and gripped the haft of her spear until her hands ached.

They swooped, and glided, keeping her pent here by circling, even as the toad things had striven to imprison her under the tree. There was a third, then a fourth cry as two more joined their fellows.

That they were hunters she knew. Their beaks and the vicious talons on their feet proclaimed the threat. Had she been caught in the open they might have borne her down easily. But they seemed in no hurry to close in as yet.

More of the birds appeared until she was beseiged by six, while a seventh kept above its fellows. It was that which now uttered the piercing cries, while the rest fell silent. Brixia began to speculate that her position was now that of a snowcat who had been brought to bay on some mountain ledge, hounds baiting it while they waited for the arrival of their master.

Who—or what—controlled the birds? The feeling of being entranced in an evil nightmare grew stronger. Was it that she still lay in slumber back under that tree which had seemed such a welcoming refuge, that this was some dream to bring about her undoing?

Dream or no she was able to feel heat, thirst, and

fear which was not that of a dream, but of a waking mind. Ever alert, she watched the birds, unable to do anything else. But she did go down on one knee to grub out of the baked earth about the foot of the rock some stones of a size to fit well into her palm. If she could bring down a leaper, then there was a chance she might also astound an over-confident bird, given a fair chance.

Brixia made a careful choice of her stones, weighing each in her hand, studying its shape. She knew the value of such caution. At length she had nine to suit her, too heavy to be considered pebbles, yet shaped well enough to throw.

The birds still coasted silently about, their shadows sweeping back and forth across the ground. While that one farther aloft continued to shriek. That answer Brixia had come to expect broke just as she arranged her last choice of stone well to hand in a hollow in the rock, a pocket from which she could scoop her ammunition and still remain standing.

That long drawn cry was not quite a match to the screams of the bird. And, as far as the girl could judge, it sounded from ground level not the air above. She fingered her spear and studied the stretch of desert immediately before her.

The stone escarpments were in greater numbers farther on, one melting in the haze against another, so sometimes she wondered if they did not, in truth, form a series of rock hills to match the mounds from which she had come. Now there was a flutter of movement by one to her left, angling up from the southwest.

That lone bird on sentry-go winged away, out toward what moved there. And again that call sounded. A human cry? Brixia could not be sure. While, even if what came to finish the hunt wore human shape, in this place such a familiar body could well encase a very alien entity. The Waste was never to be trusted to conform to the standards of Dalesmen.

Whatever did come traveled at a pace which was close to a run. And it looked human. True enough it seemed to speed upright on two legs and in form it was man-like—

Then—it took to the air. Being confronted by one of those gullies, the runner launched upward in a huge leap, throwing wide the upper limbs. Those appeared to expand, take on a wing-like outline. So supported the thing arose well into the air, flapped the arm wings, gained so a good distance, the bird flying ever above it.

It was close enough now so that the haze no longer cloaked it and Brixia knew her half-guess was right. This was no outlaw who had somehow managed to train birds as a hawker did his hunters, rather this was one of the legendary monsters of the Waste, some remnant of the Old Ones, either servant or master descended now to a seeker of meat in a heat riven land.

Master—no, mistress!

That lean body coming across the land in those huge sailing leaps, which were half short flights, was grotesquely female, there being no clothing to cover the heavy breasts, their scarlet nipples ringed about with a fringe of grayish feathers. Patches of feathers grew elsewhere on the body, aping the hair which so appeared on human frames. The head had a crest of pinions now erect. While broad, strong looking, flight feathers began at each wrist, extending rapidly in length size until at the shoulder they were near the length of the arm itself.

The features on the face were more avian than human. Eyes were deep set and the mouth and nose were united into a huge, wickedly curved, beak of a flame red color. The four fingered hands, at the ends of the wing arms, were mainly long talons well armed for rending, while the thing touched not feet to the ground between those leaps, but the true claws of a bird.

In height it topped Brixia, but its body was thin and both arms and legs merely bone with skin stretched across. As it drew nearer she could see that it also had a tail, the trailing feathers of which rippled through the air at its darting movements.

A last bound brought it to earth at a stand beyond the reach of Brixia's spear. There it paced back and forth, its head slightly on one side like that of a bird when its curiosity concerning some strange object had been thoroughly aroused.

The bird which had escorted the thing settled on a stone the size of a boulder and folded its wings. But the other six continued on sentry duty around Brixia. Now the Waste creature opened its beak and cried out— not the scream, or even the song of a bird. No, Brixia thought that the thing spoke. But to her the words, if they were such, were unintelligible.

At least it had not attacked on sight. Could it be that as alien, yes, and frightening, as this thing appeared, it might still be brought to understand that Brixia meant it no harm and was willing to go her own way? Most of the greater beasts of the wild dales, unless driven by hunger or believing that their hunting grounds were invaded, were willing to preserve an uneasy peace with a traveler who gave no overt threat. If the same held true here— At least there was no harm in trying.

Brixia tried to forget the talons, the sharp bill. She kept her spear in her right hand, attempting to make it seem that that was a staff only. Her left she raised palm out in the sign of peace which was instinctive with her own kind.

Her voice was hoarse with thirst but she used it as clearly as she might:

"Friend—friend—" she repeated the word as distinctly as possible.

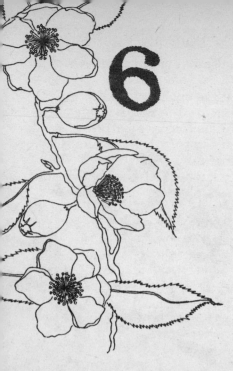

6

THE BIRD-WOMAN'S head still turned from one side to the other as if she must do so in order to focus on Brixia with one eye at a time. Now her bill-mouth opened. From it came not the earlier call but a mocking screech of what sounded close to malicious human laughter. She raised her arms high, the feathers fringing them extended so that more than ever these appeared like wings. Her talon fingers spread to their widest extent and quivered, as if eager to rake into defenseless flesh. While there was nothing remotely human in the gaze she held steadily on Brixia.

Now the seventh bird which had been perched on the tall rock a little behind its mistress arose into the air and headed straight for the girl. Brixia groped behind her with a reflex action years of facing danger had taught. Her finger closed about one of the stones she

had laid ready there and she hurled it with the best aim she could summon.

There was another screech. A noisome feather loosed from the bird, as it veered and circled on up into the air, joining those others still in their besieging ring about the outcrop.

Brixia brought the spear into readiness, expecting now to meet a forward dash from the bird-woman. But the creature delayed. Rather she hopped from one clawed foot to another in an odd jerky dance. But she no longer laughed. Nor did any of the birds drop to dive in upon Brixia.

Why they hesitated to attack the girl could not tell. Unless—her hand went to the breast of her shirt, the bud— Would the now closely closed flower of the tree which had given her shelter again provide some kind of a guard here?

Continuing to hold the spear at ready, she worked the bud out into the open. It was still tightly encased as it had been this morning, the shiny brown outer petals sealing all which had given light and perfume in the night.

But when her hand closed about it Brixia was startled. Though, instead of loosing grip because of what she had felt, rather her fingers tightened the more on it. The bud was warm—not only warm, but it pulsated in her hold. She might well have clasped a slowly beating heart!

Keeping her eyes on the bird-woman, Brixia brought the bud out and then dared to give it a quick glance. No, there was no sign of it opening. It remained tightly enfolded.

Again the bird-woman fanned her arm wings, sending the heated air of the desert to raise a portion of sand and grit, blew that, with the foul scent of her own body, directly into Brixia's face. Her jiggling dance grew faster, the claw feet in turn stirring up the surface soil in spurts of dust.

One such kick sent flying to Brixia's own face the feather which had fallen from the wing of the bird. And that did not fall back to earth. Rather it arose in the air like an arrow shot from a bow with a definite target in view.

Brixia dodged. But it was not aimed at her face as she had first thought. Instead it shot up, to lay across the fist which was shut around the bud. The strangeness of that was no natural happening, of that the girl was certain.

But did the feather come to serve some purpose of these desert hunters? She shook her hand vigorously, striving to send it flying. It did not flutter away, but remained balanced across her fist as if fastened there.

And she dared not set down her spear to pluck it off—such a move might be just what these others awaited.

A feather—

Its touch was so light on her flesh she could not be aware of its presence visually. Why—why had it come to her and in such a fashion?

The black length of it was like a giant evil finger laid across to seal the bud from the light of day.

The black length of it—

Brixia's breath caught in a gasp. Black—no! The color along the quill was changing— The black faded, became gray—

Now the bird-woman screamed, and her throat-wracking cry was picked up and echoed by all those wheeling above. The sound made Brixia jerk her head, cower back against the stone. She watched for the attack she believed that clamor must signal.

But, save for her dance, the bird-woman did not move. While the feather grew lighter and lighter. Now it was the shade of fine ashes, nearly white—

Brixia flipped her hand frantically from side to side, up and down, hoping to shake it off. To no avail. The feather was now a pearly white. Not only white, but it seemed to draw light to it in an odd way, as if a very pale radiance curved along it to be diffused at the edges. The radiance—how could one be sure of such a thing in this blaze of desert sun?

At the same time there was movement within Brixia's tight hold upon the bud as if something now struggled there for freedom. She found that a will beyond her own commanded her muscles so that her fingers began to loose the protecting grip.

Her hand moved in a high jerk, though she had not consciously ordered that. The feather loosed at last, spun upward and out and—

A bird flew up into the air. In form it was as large and

of the same shape as those which beleaguered her.
But in color this was the pearl-white of the tree flowers.
Once in the air it darted forward straight at the head of
the bird-woman.

The creature from the Waste struck at it with out-
spread wings, screamed in rage. While the birds which
served her broke their circle and came spiraling down
to where she battled with the darting flyer.

Brixia dropped her spear. Holding the bud tight to
her breast she snatched up her stones, one after
another, and flung them at the wheeling birds, and
their furiously dancing and screeching mistress. Some
thudded home. There were two of the birds fluttering
on the ground. The bird-woman gave a great cry as
one wing dropped to her side and she did not seem
able to raise it again.

But there was other movement out on the desert
land. Brixia had been so intent upon her own struggle
that she had not been conscious that a new force was
drawing in. Things scuttled about stones, moved so
quickly she could not be sure of where they went. She
only knew that this battle was now a focus for interest
and she could not hope that what came would be any
help to her.

The white bird had not attacked with either claws or
beak, thought it was as well equipped with both.
Rather it appeared to attempt to confuse and mislead
the black flock and their mistress. Illusion? There could
be no other answer Brixia thought. But whose illusion?
It had not been born of any sorcery she had worked.
She was no Wise Woman, no dealer in the forgotten
magics of the Old Ones. She—

In her mouth there was a faint taste of the healing,
nourishing bounty of the tree. And closing her in came
the scent of its flowering. She had drawn into her being
what it had had to offer—not by conscious knowledge,

but because it had seemed the natural thing to do.
What *had* flowed into her then?

"Green Mother," her voice was hardly more than a
croak, "I do not know what I have done— If I only
knew!"

Once more the bud within her hand gave a great
beat, so strong a one that it made the flesh and bone
which encased it quiver. Was that in a measure some
answer? Some reassurance? Brixia did not know what
was happening to her—nor did she have time to set
her mazed thoughts in order.

But the screaming of the birds had brought another
sound, not as an echo—rather an answer. Creatures
flashed into view, able to move so quickly that Brixia
had only a fleeting impression of supple, lengthy
bodies, either bare of any haired covering, or else scale
set. These leaped out so that the bird-woman, with a
great squawk of rage, turned to give battle. She was
not backward about action now as she had hesitated
when fronting Brixia. It was as if she had not been sure
.of what armament the girl might bring to bear while
what she wrought with now she knew well and classed
as an ancient enemy.

Escape! Was this her chance? Brixia could not tell,
but she was sure in that moment while she viewed the
whirling battle between the two parties of the desert
dwellers that she might never have another such op-
portunity. As she made up her mind to move so, once
more the bud gave a throb as if urging her on to that
course. Or it might have been in warning— But as long
as she was Brixia she was determined to follow her
own will.

Back still to the stone, she edged to the left, turning
slowly to put the outcrop between her and the struggle. At last that knob of rock did hide the skirmish from
her. Bud in one hand, spear in the other she ran—not
out into the desert but back towards the dark line of the

mounds. Whether she would bring up against the mound wall, pursued by the desert creatures to her death, she did not know. But that she had a chance if she was driven farther into the unknown she was sure could not be so.

Above her the mounds loomed, bare and dark under the westerning sun which was now well on its way down the sky behind her. There was little comfort in viewing the humps of this range. To spend a night in close contact with them was not a thing she wanted. But better that than the desert.

She passed over the rim of sand and gravel and saw before her the unyielding rise of the coarse-grassed slope. In spite of the menace of those cutting blades she would have to win up and over, put at least one of the mounds between her and the open desert. Whether the bird-woman and her flock, always supposing that they did win out in their struggle with those other things, could follow her here she did not know.

Her side pained from running as she lurched along. Hunger was a dull ache and thirst was even worse. How long she could continue to keep going she had no idea. She was not even sure that this was the place where she had come through to enter the desert—or had been herded through at a dark and alien will.

Up then—she would have to make it. Exerting what strength she had left, Brixia dug the spear deep into the mound a little above the height of her own shoulder, prepared to pull on that up the side.

She sprawled forward, slamming down on her face, so that the ill smelling soil filled her nose, squeezed between her lips. For a long moment her dazed mind could not understand what had happened. But as she fought to brace herself up she could see—

The mound she had prepared to climb—was gone! She lay in a narrow way between two arching rises of dank earth where the dying sun did little to show anything ahead but gathering shadows. The road—or a road—had opened again!

Brixia was too winded by her retreat and her fall to do more now for a moment or two than to huddle where she was, gasping for breath, smearing her hand across her muck stained face to clean it as best she could.

She had been herded through this way before— was she now going to once again follow a path which would lead her to some other trap such as the desert had nearly proven to be? If that was the truth of it—why should she hurry into some unknown danger?

So Brixia continued to stay where she was as the last rays of the sun disappeared at her back, and the shadows grew even darker and longer, to reach for her with their hungry fingers. She was trying to marshall her thoughts in order, to understand what had happened to her—if she could ever do that!

It seemed to her now that, ever since she had gone down into the ruins of Eggarsdale and been caught there in the affairs of its mind-ruined lord, she had not been herself, or the person she had learned to be in order to keep on living.

Did some Will now move her without her consent, even without her clear knowledge, to suit a purpose which was not even part of the affairs of her kind? She was all daleblood, no part of her had a trace of the Old Ones—she was not like Lord Marbon who might indeed be pliable to enscorcelment of one kind or another.

Dalesmen—and women—had been caught up, true enough, in some of the sorcery laid traps which were scattered here and there across the country to work alien wills even after the passage of centuries. Brixia from her childhood had had in plenty warnings based on those old tales, rife in any keep, concerning what might happen to any one foolish or reckless enough to go exploring in forbidden places. Men had entered for treasure and came forth blasted, dying, or were not seen again. Some with a curiosity which rode them as strongly as the greed of others pushed them, went seeking knowledge. A few found it—and then discovered that their own kin feared them and they were set apart.

Kuniggod— Not for the first time during her long wandering Brixia thought of the mystery of her old nurse. Kuniggod had been a woman of authority, ruling the House of Torgus as mistress, for Brixia had not the age nor the experience to manage the keep, and her father was cut off in one of the first battles with the invaders—his true fate never known. Since her mother had died at her birthing there was no other lady of the dale.

But—who *was* Kuniggod? She was—how *old* had she been? Brixia held memories of her nurse from her own earliest years, and Kuniggod had never seemed to age—she was always the same. Though she did not claim to be a Wise Woman with all the hidden knowledge, she had been a healer and a grower of herbs. Her garden had been the finest Brixia had ever seen. That judgment was not delivered because she herself had seen but little then beyond the boundaries of the dale.

No, travelers had marveled at it. While over the years before the invasion merchant peddlers had brought Kuniggod roots and seeds from far places. Twice a year she had gone to the Abbey at Norsdale, taking Brixia with her when she was of an age to travel. And there Kuniggod had spoken with the Abbess and her Mistress of Herb lore as an equal.

She had, as the landspeople said, "green fingers", for her plantings thrived and flourished. And at each time of sowing in the fields Kuniggod had thrown always the first handful of grain, uttering the blessing of

Gennora of the Harvests as she so gave seed to the waiting ground.

Now Brixia guessed Kuniggod had had her own secrets which she, her nurseling, had never even thought existed. Was it because she remembered something of Kuniggod's learning that the tree had welcomed her last night, given her the bud—? For that had been freely given to her Brixia was now sure.

The bud had had something to do—probably everything to do—with the change of the feather into bird. Perhaps if she were only more learned she could use it for better protection than the spear, the stones, she had come to depend upon.

Now she opened her hand and looked at the bud. But it was no longer so tightly enrolled. Those dark outer sheath petals were loosening. Through the cracks there issued a small glow. From it also came the fragrance—faint now, but still rising from the bud in her hold.

It had not withered nor faded. Clearly it was not a normal growth such as she might have picked at random from any bush or tree known to the Dales. And it was opening swiftly, the petals springing back even as she watched. While the heady perfume soothed somehow both Brixia's hunger and thirst.

She looked over the soft glow of the flower back into

the desert. The clamor of the struggle there had died away without her noticing it. She could see nothing stirring between her and the outcrop which had been her shelter.

Now, leaning on her spear as a support, she got to her feet and resolutely turned to gaze at the dark way between the mounds which had so strangely opened at her return. She went slowly, keeping moving by will alone, as her aching body answered weakly to the demands she made. But she wanted to be out of sight—and perhaps of the reach of any prowler—of the desert country before she sought shelter for the night.

As it had done when she entered the country of the mounds, so now did the open path between them twist and turn. Sometimes Brixia believed she was going north in the general direction the tracks—when Uta's paw sign had been a part of them—had led. But at other times she feared that she lost more ground in such twisting than she had gained.

However there was always a way open. While in the twilight the flower in her hand beamed the brighter, saving her from being swallowed altogether by the encroaching dark. She longed to find her way back to the tree, though she feared that that might be impossible. At length she was stumbling so badly that she knew, with a stab of uneasiness, she was nearly done.

She dropped down, a mound at her back, and stretched her aching legs out before her. The spear lay across her knees, but both of her hands, cupped, rested in her lap, and there lay the flower, now fully open, with a glimmering life of its own, pulsating as if it breathed in a fashion not unlike that which kept the air flowing in and out of her own lungs.

How long could she keep on—without food or water? She did not want to think of what it would be like to crawl on in the morning no better provided for than

she was tonight. Resolutely she set her mind to the old discipline of living for the moment only and not anticipating what disappointments or perils might lie ahead.

That she could flog her tired and fasting body to any sentry duty this night was impossible. The sleep which now weighted her lids, made her body lie limply back, could not be denied. Brixia closed her eyes on the humped mounds looming about her.

The flower lay flat open on her breast. Did its flow of light fit itself to the beating of her heart? If it did Brixia did not rouse enough to mark that. But it slowed the flare and fade of light, and the breathing, the heart beat of the sleeping girl grew calmer as she rested in a relaxation deeper than she had known for a long time.

Did she dream? Brixia could not have said yes or no. There was a confused trace of memory afterwards—of seeing Kuniggod lying in the place of the Old Ones—not dead, no—but sleeping—sleeping as to her tired body—but awake in another and more important way. And Kuniggod—or the essence of her which was more important than any body—saw Brixia. Whether she wished her good—again Brixia could not hold any dream born memory of that. But that there was something of import that passed between them—yes. Of that she was certain.

She opened her eyes. The darkness of the night was held at bay just beyond her body by the radiance of the flower. Now the sky overhead was cloud filled and curtained against even the distant sparks of the stars.

For a long moment Brixia lay so. Then whatever summons had drawn her out of slumber once more insinuated itself into her mind. She got to her knees, groped with one hand for the spear. Her body did not seem a part of her anymore—it was the need to get on which mattered.

On her feet, she started down the way. The glow of

the flower only showed a step or two beyond. What might be waiting there was hidden. Yet she must go this path and there was a reason for haste. Brixia searched for that reason within herself. Was it so needful that she catch up with those others? Or was this a subtle warning that she must not linger in a dangerous territory? What had made a trap for her once might well so work again.

There were odd sounds to be heard out of the darkness. At first she thought of the birds—and their mistress—and then of the half seen serpent-like things which had done battle with those. There were also the night ranging toads— There could be dangers in the dark so countless that no man could list them in days—and nights—of time.

Only, as she listened, the main part of what she heard came more and more to puzzle her. It was as if someone, just beyond the reach of hearing intelligible words, spoke—some one? Many voices, some high, some low and with more force. Brixia strained more and more in the hope of making out a single word, of learning whether she did catch the muted speech of her own kind. Yet if there was such company she approached it no closer even though she was walking faster, drawn on in spite of herself by the hope of finding perhaps the three that she sought.

This was as if the busy life of a dale flowed about her just beyond her ability to touch it, to make contact with what lay forever in shadow. Or was she the shadow— trapped in that fashion from the real world?

One could imagine anything in the night. Especially if one were light-headed from lack of food and water. The scent of the flower might even have addled her mind somewhat—even as the juice or fruit of some growths could drug and even send mad the unwary.

Still Brixia walked, and listened to the voices always just beyond her understanding. Once she nursed a

fancy that the mounds about her covered the ruins of
some keep and those who filled the dark with whispering sound were the soul-shadows of those who had
lived there. Such things had been known among the
legends of her people.

Oddly enough she no longer felt any fear. It was as if
the purpose which had sent her on also enveloped her
spirit, encasing her with a sense of protection. Right,
then left, the way would turn, and her feet with it. And
all around ever the darkness.

Did she walk all the rest of the night? Brixia could
never afterwards be sure—nor did she know how long
she had lain in exhausted sleep before she had started
on. One foot was set before the other mechanically
now. She did not even try to see what lay ahead, the
will which moved her superseded her own.

Nor was she aware at first that the country around
her was changing. The mounds were growing fewer,
but such as remained gave her, though she could see
little of them through the dark, a feeling of being much
higher. Then the butt of the spear which she used for a
support thudded home not on soil but on something
hard, which gave forth a ringing sound that stirred her
out of the half dream in which she moved.

Brixia raised her head. There was a dull gray in the
sky. She dropped to her knees, released a little from
the compulsion to keep on. So the light of the flower
fell directly on the ground about her. There was a wide
stretch of blocks, fitted one to the other in a manner
which could only mark a road. Across the nearest ran a
drift of soil. While planted in the midst of that, with the
firmness of something stamped with a purpose, was
the clear mark of a cat's paw.

ALMOST TIMIDLY Brixia put out a finger tip to touch that track. It was real, not some trick played by her eyes in the very dim early light. Uta—if Uta had left this sign—then she herself must have won through the trickery—at least for a time—which had been played on her. If she hurried—then surely she could find the others, she would not be lost alone in a place of witchery against which she had only a flower to use in her own defense.

Brixia wavered again to her feet and staggered forward. The flower itself was once more closing, but more slowly than it had opened. Enough light still spread from it to give her a clear sight of the path. So she continued to spy other markings surely left by Uta wherever there was patch of soil to play her guide.

The mounds no longer closed her in. Also here was something else—a stand of thorned bushes, growths she recognized. Though protected with long thorns as was the fruit still clinging to those branches, Brixia was ready to fight to fill her mouth, know the relief of the tart juice from crushed berries to ease the torment of both thirst and hunger. She ate ravenously, paying no attention to scratches as she jerked whole handfuls of

the dark globes from their stems at once. They were
poor fare, sour and small. But at that moment she
thought them better than any banquet of a high feast
day.

Not only did she eat until she was unable to swallow
more, but she pinned together some of the leaves,
plucking the thorns to do so, and filled as best she
could the unsteady bag which resulted from her
labors. There was no promise that she might have
such overwhelming luck again.

The first streamers of the sun were painting the sky
when she had done what she could to assemble her
supplies. So having recruited her strength somewhat,
she now gave a more detailed survey to the land
around her.

Whether or no the mounds through which she had
come had been the remains of some ancient ruins,
there was evidence enough around that she did follow
a way of the Old Ones. Traces of walls projected here
and there, and it was plain that a paved road stretched
ahead to where some heights greater than the
mounds, stood dark against the sky northward.

Since Uta's tracks pointed in that direction it was
where she must go, much as her fast awakening distrust of everything to do with the Waste made her
wary. There was no "feel" to this place, however—
she sensed neither the peace and welcome which lay
about some of the old remains, nor the warning shrinking which was the foretaste of evil to come. The road
ran straight ahead, its blocks easy to see, though
covered in parts with soil in which grass, even bushes,
had taken root to cloak it.

By the clear light of day Brixia faced those higher
hills and went forward, but not without such caution as
she had learned, until she reached those hills. Like the
mounds they were covered with grass, dull green and
rather withered looking. While these were only the first

of a barrier of rises which grew taller and taller ahead. The road headed straight towards a break between two of the hills.

On either hand stood a pillar of stone. These towered high enough to match the crowns of the wailing hills. The pillars were square with eroded corners, bearing the same signs of great age as had the carvings on the cliff she had descended into the Waste. On the tops had been set figures.

To the right, in spite of the wear of wind and weather, was a representation of a toad thing. It had been fashioned, with unmistakable menace and perhaps warning, in a crouching position as if about to leap from its post to bar the path.

While opposite, not facing outward, as did the threatening toad, but across the gap, staring slit-eyed at its fellow, was a cat. The figure was seated in the same quiet fashion which Uta often chose, the tip of its tail folded neatly over forepaws. It displayed no dark promises similar to the toad's threat, rather a suggestion of curious interest.

Viewing the toad Brixia's hand went to her breast, to press against the now closed blossom from the tree. She was not surprised at an answer to that pressure, the feeling of gentle warmth against her skin.

Once beyond the pillars, the road narrowed so that if she stretched her arms as far apart as she might, her finger tips would brush, on either side, the sides of the hills.

Brixia was aware of something else. Though she tried to keep to her steady pace, here she went more slowly. Not by any desire, but with the odd feeling that, with each step she took, she was wading through unseen, adhesive muck which sought to detain her. So shortly her effort to advance became more and more of a struggle.

The hunger which the berries had only in part stilled was again gnawing at her, thirst as well. Her bruised feet hurt, the crude sandals having not protected them over well. Water—food—the hurt of her feet—her body sagged more and more, demanding relief for its needs.

At the same time that other sense of clarity, of oneness with the world, which had been with her from the mornings she had awakened under the tree, was returning to be a spur. Perhaps it was a warning that the needs of her flesh must in no way master her now.

Brixia continued on with dogged stubbornness. Above her the slice of sky was clear of any cloud. But full beams of the morning sun were shut out and a chill spread from the hillsides. The girl shivered, and often she glanced behind her. A feeling that she was being followed grew stronger with every breath she drew. Perhaps some creature from the desert dogged her just out of sight. She looked often to the sky, fearing to see a sweep of black wings there. Always she listened—sure that sooner or later she might hear the gibbering of the toad things, or that confused muttering which had accompanied her through the mound land.

As she watched so intently for what lay both before and behind her, Brixia sighted more paw signs left by Uta. Always they were on the hillside to her left, stretching behind cat marker.

What part had Uta's people long ago played in the Waste? Brixia had seen from time to time fragments of Old Ones' working—small figures, grotesque, few of them beautiful—some amusing, but many disturbingly ugly, most of species unknown to the Dales people. There had been a few representations of horses, one or two of hounds (though with odd peculiarities which no Dale dog matched), but never had she seen a cat. In fact Brixia had always believed those had been, as the Dales people themselves, newcomers into a land the Old Ones had largely deserted.

Still it was plain that the sculptured cat on the pillar must be as old as its toad companion. Therefore Uta herself might have come, from no pillaged homestead or keep as Brixia had believed, but out of the Waste. If so— To trust anything out of the Waste was folly.

Slower and slower grew the girl's pace, for with each step that struggle against the unseen pressure sharpened. Her mouth was dry again so much so a handful of the bruised berries brought no ease. Water—a spring—a brook— Could such be found here? Or was the Waste indeed mostly desert, its sources of water secrets known only to the life which crept, flew, walked here?

The thought of water strengthened its hold upon her mind. She had vivid mental pictures of small pools, of a spring breaking out of the earth.

Water—

Brixia's head came up, turned sharply right. She was sure she could not mistake that tantalizing sound. Water—running—just over the hill. She faced the steep rise. Just over the hill, or she certainly could not hear it so clearly! Water—her tongue rasped across her dry lips.

Then—

Heat—heat as searing as a glowing iron laid upon bare flesh. She uttered a small cry, clutched at her breast. Under the shirt—

Tearing upon her clothing she examined her body. The flower! Though the tight bud it had returned to this morning had not again opened, it was once more emitting a light which she could see in this dusky way. Not only light, but a strong heat which she had not felt even when she had fronted the bird-woman.

Brixia brought out the bud. The heat it generated did not lessen. Light streamed from the very tip where the ends of the petals folded against each other, a small thread of light reminding her once again of the wick of a burning candle.

On impulse she held the bud closer to the slope she had been about to climb. The light flared, and with that came a surge of heat so intense she might have dropped the bud had she not half suspected such a reaction might occur.

The girl bit her lip. The heat—a warning? She had asked a question in her mind, and that burning flare seemed to leave answered that peril awaited there. But was there water? Now she strained to hear that sound which had been so loud and luring—

It had ceased. Bait for another snare—a trap—? With the bud in the open where she could look upon it so, that reassuring feeling of oneness with the world took an upsurge. Yes, her confidence grew as might a plant in rich earth, well fostered by care.

So the water sound *was* a trap! Set by whom for whom? Brixia did not think this one set for her—rather it must be one placed long ago—perhaps forgotten, but still working, though the trapper had departed.

She thirsted still; only when she held the bud before her eyes her desires lessened—flesh did not command spirit. The bud must not be hidden but used as the spear, the worn knife, a defense as powerful as either.

However, Brixia discovered that even if the flower could reveal the trap, it was less efficient against that curious pull which kept her walking against the counter feeling of unseen obstruction. Though all men knew magic was both lesser and greater. Some spells, they declared, might move mountains and change the world, and others could scarce lift a pebble. Thus the bud might be a talisman against one danger and little or no aid against another.

The light from its tip did not die. That fact heartened her as the hills grew higher, the way between more and more shadowed. To see the sky now she must strain her head far back on her shoulders and stare directly up.

Ahead the rearing hills came together, forming a high wall. But the path did not end, rather it fed into a dark opening. The arch over that was of stone, set and fitted as if to support a door. No such barrier hung there, however. The way was wide open, yet it did not welcome.

Brixia paused. Her flesh tingled, the light of the bud was brighter, flaring up. This was—a place of Power! Though she had no training as a Wise Woman, she was able to sense that even without such learning— one could feel the out-reaching of this kind of Power in one's body.

But there were powers and powers. All the world was balanced, light against dark, good against evil. So it was with the Powers—and the Dark could be as powerful and conquering in some places as the Light was in others. Which did she face now? She sniffed for the taint of evil—tried to open some illusive inner sense to give her warning.

She had only the flower on which to build her frail hopes. It and the tree from which it sprung had saved her before. That the toad things who tried to net her with their sorcery were of the Dark Brixia had not the slightest doubt. And the flower had been her defense in the desert as well as protecting her only a short time ago from the enchantment of the promised water, working even here in a place which she had begun to think was tainted with a trace at least of evil.

In truth she had no choice—that compulsion which had brought her into the Waste grew ever stronger as she journeyed. Try as she might now she could go no way except ahead.

Step by halting step Brixia approached the mouth of the doorway. If the light of the bud only continued— the *bud*? In her hold the flower was once again opening. The girl hurriedly flattened her palm, allowing it room for the petals to unfurl. From those arose that clean and cleansing scent, while the light grew ever stronger.

Still engrossed in the wonder of that new blooming, she passed beneath the stone arch, into a way which would have been as utterly dark as the secret passage of the keep had she not had the flower to hearten her.

The walls were of dressed stone. Within a few paces of the entrance these became dankly damp with trickling moisture. Thirsty as Brixia was, she could not bring herself to attempt to catch that. For the drops were thick and oily, as if formed by unwholesome liquid oozing through the crevices.

Fighting against the dank smell was the fragrance of the flower. Not for the first time Brixia wondered how long the blossom might last before withering. She marveled that such fading had not yet begun.

Deeper and deeper bored the passage. By the light of her flower-torch she saw paw marks on the floor. So the others or at least Uta, were still before her.

What did Lord Marbon seek? To his disordered wits had that old doggerel he had sung become a truth he must prove? If so he might push on, uncaring, until he dropped, worn out by the demands of a body which he did not rest nor tend. Or would the boy be able to break through that web of confusion, and, sooner or later, rescue his lord?

Zarsthor's bane—Brixia shaped the words with her lips but did not repeat them aloud. What was Zarsthor's Bane? There were tales a-many about lost talismans—things of power which could grant their possessors this or that favor—or in turn bring about this or that fate. It would seem that Zarsthor's Bane was of the latter sort. Then why did Marbon seek it? To bring revenge on his enemy?

The war was over. Even to such wanderers as Brixia had drifted the news that the invaders had been driven back until, caught between the bitter hatred of the Dalemen and the sea, they had been ground into nothingness. Outlaws there were in plenty, and scavengers out to loot and kill where no lord could marshall a force to beat them off. This was a blasted land in which each man's hand was raised in suspicious against his fellow. There might be many reasons for a man to long for a "bane" to use as a weapon.

She wondered how far ahead of her the others now were. If man and boy and cat had pushed on they might be a whole day's tramp ahead. But surely they must have rested—

There was a scuttling noise. The thin radiance of the flower was reflected by two sparks of greenish light near the floor. Brixia paused, took a firmer grip on her spear. She held the flower out, stooping a little, striving to catch a glimpse of what moved there.

A narrow head upraised. This creature was not unlike the lizard she had seen perched upon the rock when she first entered the Waste. It was not one of the foul toads to be feared. When the beam of flower light touched it, the thing did not flee, as she had half expected. Rather it strained to hold its head higher, and that weaved back and forth on a supple neck. Its jaws parted and a tongue flickered at her. There sounded a hiss, as it backed a little away. Keeping always the same distance from her, it made no other move to either advance or retreat.

"Haa—" she uttered that, hoping her voice might banish it when light did not. Though the creature did not seem large enough to be a threat, she could not tell if it were poisonous.

Her voice did not send it into hiding either. Instead the lizard paused and reared. Now she could see it was six-legged—different from a lizard of the outer world. It balanced on the four hind feet, lacking any length of tail save a stub jutting from the hind quarters. The two forepaws were oddly shaped—more like her own hands, the clawed digits resembling fingers. These dangled over its lighter underbelly as it watched her.

Brixia stood still. Lizards could move with lightning speed. She doubted whether she could counter any attack with her spear. Though when it was erect it stood no taller than her knee, so size and weight were in her favor. Her best hope was perhaps the flower.

"I mean no harm—" Why she spoke to the creature the girl did not know, the words came from her much as those others had when she addressed the tree. "I only wish to pass this way, seeing that it is set upon me that I must. Remain free from any harm from me, scaled one."

The tongue no longer flickered. Instead the narrow head cocked a little to one side, the unblinking beads of eyes regarded her, as Uta was wont to do, with a measuring stare.

"I am no unfriend to you and your kin. By this gift of the Green Mother," she stooped farther, holding the flower still lower and closer to the lizard one, "see that I am without harm."

A tongue, seeming so long that it could not be furled within the space of the creature's mouth, lashed forward, held for a moment but finger distance from the flower, snapped back into hiding once more. Still balanced upon the two pair of hind feet, the thing edged away to the left wall of the passage, leaving open the way immediately before her. Brixia believed she understood.

"My thanks to you, scaled one," she said softly. "Whatever you desire—may that thing be yours."

She walked by the upright creature, schooling herself to show no apprehension. To it she must convey that she accepted without question what it offered, free passage without harm.

Nor did she allow herself to quicken her pace. If the creature was of the true Dark, then the flower had again proven its worth as a safeguard. If the lizard were

allied perhaps to the Light, the blossom must have been her passport.

The way continued and Brixia wondered how large a hill she did traverse, for the way had neither dipped nor arisen, but ran straight. Though there was no gravel here to cut the sadly worn wrappings on her feet, the soles burned and ached, and she was tired. Still, to rest in this dark pocket—no, that she could not bring herself to do.

At last she limped once more into the open. What she saw was a valley shaped like a huge basin, high lands marking its rim, sloping gently downward. Nor could she detect from where she now stood any visible break in that wall of the heights.

What meant the most to her was that the center of the vale cupped a stretch of water. On that part of the bank closest to her burned a fire from which a thin thread of smoke arose. Up from the edge of the water came the boy. Of Lord Marbon she could see nothing—unless he lay in the tall growing grass.

Water more than company drew her stumbling on. She halted once to tuck the closing flower back into hiding under her shirt. Then again using her spear as a support she went on; gaining some relief from the soft grass underfoot.

She was half the distance toward the lake when Uta appeared out of the grass beside her. The cat mewed a loud welcome before, turning, she matched pace with Brixia's, escorting her toward the small camp. But the boy did not equal Uta's friendliness.

"Why do you come?" His hostility was as open as it had been at their first meeting.

The words with which Brixia answered him came not from any conscious thought at all. It was almost as if they had been dictated by another.

"There must be three—three to search—and one—one to find and lose."

Lord Marbon heaved himself up from where he had indeed been lying near, concealed in the grass. He did not look to her, rather replied as if her words had stirred him again into either partial memory or coherent thought:

"Three must be—and the fourth— It is so. Three to go—one to reach outside— It is truly so."

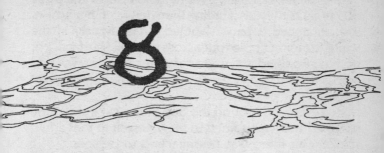

THE BOY SNARLED.

"Do you dare to strengthen him in this haunted dreaming then?" he spat at Brixia. "No word of reason from me has reached him since he came through the escape way. He would have only the Bane and will drive himself to death for it."

No word of reason had reached him, perhaps, yet Lord Marbon's face no longer was empty, vacant. But his eyes were not for them at all, rather he watched the lake eagerly—almost demandingly. A frown of puzzlement drew his dark brows closer together.

"It is here—yet it is not—" There was a querulous note in his voice. "How can a thing be and yet not be? For this is not of idle legend, I do stand in Zarsthor's land!"

The boy continued to scowl at Brixia. "See?" he demanded. "Through the night and day he would come here, as if he knew this place as well as once he knew Eggarsdale. Now it is as if he seeks some place he knows well—but he will not tell me what!"

Uta left the girl, padded forward to the edge of the lake. The water was not rimmed by any growth of weed or plant. There was only a sharp line of light sandy earth enclosing it as far as they could see—an oval green-blue gem set in an unnaturally clearly marked tarnished casing of silver.

The cat looked back over her shoulder at the three of them. Daintily, as if urging them to watch her action, she advanced a paw, dabbled it fastidiously in the water, sending ripples out across the quiet surface. For nothing troubled that mirror of water. No insect skated across its surface, no fish sent bubbles upward to break.

Brixia limped around the boy to the cat's side. She dropped her spear, knelt to view herself in that liquid mirror. But there was no reflection to be seen.

At first glance the water was turgid, unclear below its quiet surface. It was not muddied, for the color was not brown or yellow. Brixia cautiously advanced her own hand, felt the liquid, which was slightly warm, wash up around her fingers. Withdrawing those quickly she examined them. There was no staining of any kind left on her sun-browned skin. And, when she held her hand close to her noise, there was no smell either that she could detect.

Yet it was plain the lake was not normal, judged by Dale standards. As she leaned forward again, striving to see what might indeed lie below, the bud fell out of her shirt. Though she grabbed, it had already floated just beyond her reach.

She had lifted her spear in an effort to hook it back to her when the boy cried out.

"What—what is happening?"

For, as the bud floated out upon the water, it did not appear to drift at random. Rather it moved steadily away from the shore, spinning in a spiral path. Where it passed the water cleared. The color remained, but the depths beneath could now be seen.

Below that now transparent surface were rising walls, domes. Caught within the filled cup of the lake there lay some settlement, or perhaps only a single spreading edifice, of strangely shaped building.

Out and on swirled the bud, and clearer grew what

its passage uncovered. There were carvings on the sunken walls and the glint of other colors subdued by the hue of the water. Farther in towards the center the building stretched. Nor did it show any sign of ruin or erosion.

"An-Yak!"

Brixia, startled by the shout, only saved herself from falling forward into the embrace of the lake by clutching at the long grass.

"Lord!"

Marbon passed her in a single long stride, halting only when the water washed waist high about him, his hands stretched towards lay beyond. The boy splashed after, trying to drag him back.

"No, Lord!"

Marbon fought to wade deeper into that flood. He did not even look at his companion, his attention was all for what the floating bud had disclosed.

"Let me go!" He flung the boy away. But Brixia, who had found her balance, came to seize the man's shoulders from behind. In spite of his fight to free himself, she held on as the boy came to aid her.

Somehow they dragged him out of the lake. Then he collapsed so that they had to support him between them, pull him back to the fire. Over his now inert body Brixia spoke to the boy.

"It is only because he is weak that we could master him," she pointed out. "I doubt if we can force him away from this place."

The boy had gone down on his knees to touch his lord's face.

"I know. He—he is ensorcelled! What was that which you threw into the water? It was that which caused—"

Brixia stood away. "I threw nothing. It fell from my shirt. As to what it was—a flower. One which served me well." She told him curtly of what aid she had had from the tree, and, in turn, its blossom.

"Who knows what manner of thing is to be found in the Waste?" she ended. "Much of the Old Ones' owning and rearing may be here still. Your lord named that," she waved towards the water. "Is it what he has sought then? The place of the Bane in truth?"

"How do I know? He has been one possessed, giving me no choice but to follow after. He has walked without rest, would not eat or drink when I tried to stop him. He is walled away in his own thoughts, and who may guess what those may be?"

Brixia glanced back at the lake. "It is plain that he cannot easily be kept from what lies there. Nor do I think that together we can carry him away while his senses have left him."

The boy's hands tightened into fists, and with them he pounded on the ground, his face twisted with both fear and concern.

"It is true—" his voice was very low as if he did not want to acknowledge that to her but the words were forced from him. "I do not know what I can do. Before he has been as a child I could lead, not my lord. I brought him to Eggarsdale for I thought that there his wits might return to him. Now he has brought me here—and within his mind he is as far from me as if the sea runs between us. He is ensorcelled, and I know not how to break this bond upon him. I know nothing which is of any use. Only what he has said of this Bane. Though the matter of that is still his secret." He covered his face with his hands.

Brixia bit her lip. It was close to nightfall now. She looked around with a wanderer's sharp valuation of the land. Here there stood no trees, nothing to give them any shelter at all. The fire burned on a stretch of gravel, but there were not even rocks to provide a barricade. She could no longer see the bud—if it still floated it must now be near the center of the lake.

The girl did not like the thought of being in the open when dark at last closed in. But she could sight no better camp than where they now were. Slowly she went back to the side of the lake.

Thirst parched her throat. Though she feared that stretch of water, and perhaps even more what it covered, Brixia knelt and scooped up a palm's hold of it, setting her lips gingerly to the liquid. It had no taste, no scent her human senses could detect. Uta crouched beside her and was busy lapping. Dared she depend upon the cat to point out danger here?

The few drops she had sucked from her hand were not enough. With a fatalistic shrug the girl scooped up more and drank, then splashed handfuls to wet the tangled hair on her forehead, drip from her chin. It refreshed her, in a way renewed her determination to withstand whatever might come.

Gazing over the lake she half expected to see that the murkiness had returned, to once more hide the structures below. But that was not so, she could still trace wall, dome, roof, on and on outward. Nearly below her lay a paved way which ran straight ahead into the heart of the walls.

A smell of roasting meat drew her back to the fire. There the boy tended a skinned and quartered leaper he had impaled on sticks to sizzle over the flames.

"Is he asleep still?" Brixia nodded at Lord Marbon.

"Asleep—or entranced. Who can say which? Eat if you wish," he spoke roughly, not facing her.

"You are of his House?" she asked turning the nearest of those chunk loaded sticks to roast its burden more evenly.

"I was fostered in Eggarsdale." He still looked into the flames. "As I told you, I am younger son to the Marshal of Itsford—my name is Dwed." He shrugged. "Perhaps there remains none now to call me by it. Itsford was long since swept away. You have seen

Eggarsdale—it is dead as the man who marched from it."

"Jartar—?"

Both their heads turned. Lord Marbon had raised himself on one elbow. His eyes were fixed on Brixia. She would have denied at once that she was whom he looked to see there, but Dwed's hand shot forth and his fingers closed with crushing pressure on her wrist. She guessed then what he would have her do—let her pretend to his lord, and, perhaps through such a pretense, Marbon might be drawn away from the trap of the lake. Or else be led to explain his preoccupation with it. Making her voice as low as she could, Brixia replied:

"My lord?"

"It is even as you said it might be!" His face was eager, alight. "An-Yak! Have you seen it—within the lake?" Lord Marbon sat up. There was a new youth in him, and Brixia realized how much this animation made of him a different man.

"It is there," she kept her answers as short as possible, lest some mistaken word of hers return him again to the state that had held him for so long.

"Just as the legend—the legend you spoke of," Marbon nodded. "If it is there—then also within it must lie the Bane—and with that—yes, with that!" He brought his hands together with force. "What shall we do with it, Jartar? Call down the moon to give us light? Or the stars? Be as the Old Ones themselves? Surely there is no limit for he who can command the Bane!"

"There is still a lake between us and it," Brixia said softly. "There is ensorcellment here, Lord."

"Surely," he nodded. "But there must also be a way." He glanced up at the steadily darkening sky. "Anything which is of value does not come easily to a man. We shall find a way—with the coming of light we shall do so!"

"Lord, without strength a man may do nothing," Dwed had withdrawn one of the meat laden sticks and held it out to Marbon. "Eat and drink. Be ready for what you would do with the day."

"Wise words," Lord Marbon took the stick, then he frowned slightly, studying the boy's face, revealed as it was by the firelight. "You are—are—Dwed!" He brought out the name with triumphant emphasis. "But—how—" He shook his head slowly, a measure of the old lost emptiness returning. "No!" now his voice was sharp again, "you are in foster ward—you joined us last autumntide."

Dwed's scowl was gone, he wore an eager, hopeful expression.

"Yes, my lord. And—" He caught himself nearly in mid-word. "And—" it was obvious he strove to change the subject, "since we came here, lord, you have not made plain what the nature of this 'Bane' is we seek."

Brixia was pleased at his cleverness. As long as Marbon appeared shaken out of his apathy it was well to learn as much as they could.

"The Bane—" Marbon replied slowly. "It is a tale—Jartar knows it best. Tell the lad, brother—" He turned his attention to Brixia.

So her would-be cleverness had been a mistake after all. She tried to think of the words of the doggerel song she had heard in the keep courtyard of Eggarsdale.

"It is a song, Lord, an old one—"

"A song, yes. But we have proved it true. There lies An-Yak, water buried, it proves the truth. We have found it! Tell us of the Bane, Jartar. It is the story of my House and yours, you know it best."

Brixia was trapped. "Lord, it is your tale also. You have claimed it."

He watched her narrowly from across the fire. "Jartar," he did not answer her question but asked one of his own, "why do you call me 'lord'? Are we not foster-kin?"

To that Brixia could find no answer.

"You are not Jartar!" Marbon flung the spitted meat from him. Before she could get to her feet he was around the fire, moving with a cat's grace, a cat's leaping speed. His hands had closed on her shoulders, jerking her up to face him.

"Who are you?" He shook her with force, but now she resisted. Her own hands closed about his wrists and she exerted all the strength she could summon to break his hold. "Who are you!" he demanded the second time.

"I am myself—Brixia—" She kicked at his shin and gasped at the pain in her bruised foot. Then she gave a quick sidewise fling of the head and set her teeth in his wrist with the same wild fury Uta might have shown when resenting rough handling.

He yelled and hurled her from him so that she fell into the grass. But there was enough outrage and strength in her to roll frantically away, scramble to her feet. Her spear lay beside the fire, but she had her belt knife ready in her hand.

Only he had not followed her. Instead he swayed, and he held up his wrist, eyeing the marks her teeth had left. Now he looked at Dwed who was beside him.

"I—where is Jartar? He was here—and then— sorcery! There is sorcery— Where is Jartar—why did he wear the look of—of—"

"Lord, you have slept and dreamed! Come and eat—"

Brixia saw Dwed's hold tighten on him. Perhaps the boy could soothe Marbon. In any case she had better stay well beyond the fire lest the sight of her again cause trouble. She eyed the meat hungrily.

Dwed succeeded in calming Marbon. He persuaded

the man to reseat himself, got him to pulling the seared meat from the stick to eat. Indeed the awareness had ebbed out of Marbon's eyes, his mouth became loose and slack—the forceful person he had been vanished.

Brixia watched the boy persuade his lord to settle once more to sleep. And when some time had passed without any movement in that recumbent figure the girl crept back to reach for the charred meat, gulping it down only half chewed. Dwed's voice came cold:

"He will not accept you. Why do you not go your own way—"

"Be assured that I shall," she snapped. "I tried to play your game, that good would come of it. If evil has chanced instead it is through no fault of mine."

"Good or ill—we are better apart. Why did you follow—you are no liege of his."

"I do not know why I followed," she said frankly. "I only know that something I do not understand willed it."

"Why did you speak of the three together when you came?" he persisted.

"Again I cannot answer. The words were not mine, I did not know what I said until I spoke so. There is sorcery in old places—" She shivered. "Who may say how that will influence the unwary?"

"Then be not unwary!" he snapped. "Be not here at all! We do not want you—and he may be beyond my control if he thinks you keep Jartar from him in some fashion."

"Who is this Jartar—or was he—for I heard you name him dead—that he so moved your lord?"

Dwed shot a quick glance at the sleeping man as if he feared his lord might wake to hear, then he answered:

"Jartar was my lord's foster brother—they were closer than many who are blood-kin. I know not from what House he came—though he was a man who was used to authority of his own. How can I find words to say so another can understand if that other knew not Jartar? He was no master of any Dale, yet anyone meeting with him gave him the honor name of 'lord' upon their first speaking. I think there was something strange about his past. My lord, too—men said of him that he was of mixed blood—that he had ties with the *Others*. If that was so of him, then it might be doubly so of Jartar. He knew things—strange things!

"I saw him once—" Dwed swallowed and paused, "if you say this is not possible," now he stared at her fiercely, "you give me the open lie for I saw it. Jartar spoke to the sky—and there came a wind which drove upon the enemy, forcing them into the river. Afterwards he was white and shaking, so weak my lord needs must hold him in his saddle."

"It is said that those of Power when they use it to a great degree are so weakened," Brixia commented. Nor did she doubt that Dwed had seen exactly what he reported. There were many stories of what the Old Ones could do when and if they wished.

"Yes. And he could heal—Lonan had a wound which would not close, but kept ever breaking open. Jartar went out by himself and came back with leaves which he crushed and laid upon the raw flesh. Then he sat with his hands upon the leaves, holding them there, and he stayed for a long time thus. The next day the slash began to close—there was no foul odor. It healed without even a scar. My lord could do so also—it was a gift which made him different from other men."

"But Jartar died—" Brixia said.

"He died like any other of us—by a sword thrust through the throat. For he stood above my fallen lord beating off that scum who spilled rocks into the pass to stun us. He took a wound, blood ran as it would from any man, and he died, my lord unknowing. From a

rock blow on the head, my lord came back to me with disordered wits—as you see him. Only he spoke of Jartar as one who waited somewhere for him, and that he must gain the Bane. First he said that it was because of Jartar he must do this thing—now—you have heard him! I know no more of what he seeks than that song he will sing and some scattered words.

"When he came to *this* place he walked as does a man who is so intent upon what he must do that he looks neither right nor left, but presses forward that it be speedily finished. Now it seems he has taken it into his head that what he seeks lies out there—" Dwed motioned to the lake now hidden in the night. "I know not how to deal with him any more. At first he was weak of body from the head wound and I could lead him, take care of him. Now his strength has returned. At times it is as if I am not with him at all—he thinks only of something I do not know and cannot understand."

Dwed's words spilled out as if he found relief in talking of the burden he carried. But that he expected any reponse or sympathy from Brixia—no, he would probably resent that she had heard so much after he had obtained relief from such unguarded speech.

"I cannot—" she began.

"I need no help!" Dwed was quick to refuse what she might offer. "He is my lord. As long as he lives, or I do, that will not alter. If he is under some spell—this damned land may well have set its shadow upon him forever, weak and open as his mind is. If that is so I must find what I can to break him free."

He turned his back on her and went to settle beside his lord, pulling over Marbon the journey cloak. Brixia huddled on her own side of the fire. She was very tired. Dwed might want her gone, her own sense of self preservation might agree. But tonight she could not summon strength to move on.

There was no feeling this night of being guarded, or lying safe, as there had been under the trees. The girl curled in the grass and suddenly there was a warm and purring body next to hers. Uta had come to share her bed once again. Brixia stroked the length of the cat's body from prick-eared head to smooth furred haunch.

"Uta," she whispered, "what sort of a coil have you led me into, for indeed the first meeting with these two was of your doing and I may be undone because of it."

Uta's purring was a song to weight the eyelids of the listener. Though all she had learned in the past dark years urged her to caution and to the safeguards she had always depended upon, Brixia could not rouse herself again. She slept.

"Where is he?"

She struggled out of deep sleep, a little dazed. Hands pawed at her, shook her. She opened her eyes. Dwed had hold upon her. His look was that of an enemy peering at her over a battle shield.

"Where is he—you outlaw slut!"

His hand rose, cracked against her cheek, rocking her head.

Brixia jerked back.

"Mad—you're mad!" she gasped and clawed farther along the ground, away from him.

When she was able to sit up she saw him running from the burnt out ashes of the fire down to the edge of the lake.

"Lord—Lord Marbon—!" His cry arose like a wounded man's scream. He splashed into the water, beating out frantically with his arms.

Brixia began to understand. Only Dwed and she—both Marbon and Uta were not in sight. In the same instant she knew the reason for Dwed's present fear. Had his lord awakened—walked on into that stretch of water as he had tried to do last night—walked out to death beneath the surface?

She followed Dwed to the lake's edge. That clarity which the water had gained from the passage of the bud was lost again. There was no sighting of what lay beneath its surface, smooth and quiet as a mirror save for where Dwed splashed and sought to swim. Swim he could not—just so far was he able to win into the water—then, as frantically as he struggled, he could go no further.

He was fighting in that fruitless manner when Uta broke from the grass and came unto the narrow strip of sand shore. The cat meowed, loudly and demandingly, a cry Brixia knew of old. Uta sought attention.

"Dwed—wait—!"

At first he might not have heard her, then he turned. Brixia pointed to the cat.

"Watch!" she ordered, with, she hoped, enough force to make him obey.

Uta turned and bounded off, looking back now and then to see if she were indeed being followed. Brixia broke into a trot to keep up. There was no more splashing; she glanced back. Dwed had come out of the lake, was pounding after them.

So the three of them ran on through the grass until they came to where Lord Marbon stood in a channel, dry, but cut deep enough in the soil of the valley to hide his hunched figure from their view until they were directly upon him. By his side lay Brixia's spear, earth stained, and in his hands was Dwed's sword. With the point of that he pried at a wall of stones which stopped the end of the channel.

A dam—a dam set to lock up the lake! Now he glanced at them.

"Get busy!" his voice was sharp with impatience, "don't you see—we must let the water flow. It is the only way to reach An-Yak now!"

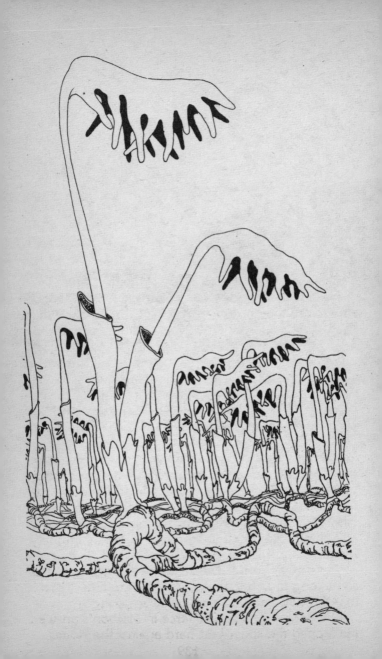

9

"LORD MARBON!"

He looked around, his dark head bare, his face once more with the life of intelligence to bring back that aspect of youth. So he was able to understand her summons. Brixia pointed to the wall he assaulted. His efforts there were already being rewarded, for water oozed through between the stones in patches of wet.

"You pull those free without more thought," the girl observed, "and it will be as taking a stopper from a filled water-skin. A whole flood will rush forth against you."

Marbon glanced back at the wall, raised his arm to draw across over a face streaked with the sweat summoned by his efforts. Then he studied the dam with narrowed eyes. Now he had the appearance of a man who might be moved by sorcery, but one who could also think for himself in some things and with judgment.

"It is true, Lord," Dwed jumped down into that same long dry channel to stand beside him. "Break that through and you may be swept away."

"Perhaps—" there was force in Marbon's answer. He tapped the spear butt hard against the stones.

By Brixia's guess there were already more patches of moisture than there had been even seconds ago.

"Lord Marbon—Dwed—get out—!" she cried. "It is beginning to give!"

Hardly knowing what she did, the girl went to her knees, leaned down to catch at Marbon's arm—since he was the nearer—snatching her spear from him. Then, throwing the weapon behind her, she tightened her hold on the man himself. Dwed moved in on his other side, exerting his strength to urge his lord towards the bank.

For a moment Marbon resisted them both. His attention was all for the wall. Then he shook free of Dwed, pulled himself up beside the kneeling girl.

"Up with you!" Marbon, too, was on his knees, reaching out to catch at Dwed's mail shirt near the neck. Setting his hold firmly, he jerked the boy towards them both. Together they pulled Dwed out of the channel just in time.

The patches on the stones thickened to trickles of water. Then one, and a second, spouted out as pressured streams to shoot beyond the foot of the dam, dashing on into the channel.

"Away—!" Marbon's arms swept out, sweeping both Brixia and Dwed with him, back from the lip of the cut. They stumbled, dragged themselves farther off. There was a sound— Brixia, edging around without getting to her feet, saw water fountain up above the banks. The whole dam must have given away suddenly.

Lord Marbon was on his feet, striding back toward the foaming river he had unloosed, Dwed close behind him. Even Uta crouched near the rim of the channel, peering down at the rushing waters.

That flood did not go far, Brixia saw as she joined the rest of the party. The rise in the slope of the valley might well have sent the draining water back towards the lake. Instead the new stream disappeared not far away. Lord Marbon had moved to that point, was looking down at the swirling, foam topped whirl pond.

"Underground," he murmured— "a river underground."

However, he spared but little attention to that. Rather he hurried back to the lake itself.

The water poured away in a steady, rushing outflow. Already a pinnacle arose out of the lake. The top of a dome showed, then another.

"An-Yak, the long-hidden—" Lord Marbon's loud cry of triumph arose above the rushing of the water. "Three and one—we have come to find what has long been lost and vainly sought!"

Still the water drained. Walls rose clear and dripping. Brixia could see that what stood here was unlike any other structure she had ever seen. Those walls now coming into view enclosed spaces for which there was no indication roofs had ever existed. There were two domes at the heart of that maze of walls, between them a slender tower, standing not very tall—perhaps less than the height of a manor watchtower. As the waters fell to disclose more and more, Brixia blinked and rubbed her eyes.

There was something very curious about what Lord Marbon named An-Yak. The sprawling structures were small—they might have been viewing it from a distance so perspective reduced the normal size. She could not explain this strangeness—only she herself felt large—too large—a giant near buildings devised for a much shorter race.

The toad people had been small—and a statue of their kind had guarded the way to An-Yak. Was this some ancient dwelling of theirs—a temple perhaps? Brixia half expected to see one of those warty, tendril haired heads break above the surface of the rapidly dwindling water.

Matching the color of flood itself, the hues of those buildings were both green and blue. Nor were those colors constant in shade. Rather, across the wet surfaces those rippled, light and dark, dark and light.

Wide bands of metal of a deep green encircled the domes. Those were set with what might be gem stones; for, catching the sun's full light, they flashed with fire. It would seem that long immersion had in no way either eroded or encrusted what had been built here.

The flood dwindled at long last. There was still a cupping of water in the middle of the lake, washing about the foundations of the walls, but no more fed on into the channel.

"An-Yak's heart—!!" Marbon leaped from the rim of the lake. As he moved purposefully forward water washed about his ankles, then arose half way to his knees.

Brixia cried out. Claws struck her shoulders, pierced her shirt, to catch in her flesh. She put up her hands to

grasp Uta, settling the cat into her arms. Dwed was already splashing after his lord and it seemed that Uta urged her to follow, perhaps looking to Brixia to provide a way for the cat to reach the once drowned building dry footed.

Her feeling that the proportions of the building before them (for she had decided that it was indeed joined together to form a single structure) were wrong continued. Its small size seemed to be normal, her own in relation to it, too large and clumsy. Water washed lazily around her feet and—

A small wavelet, set up by the passing of the two ahead, broke against her own legs. In it— Settling Uta more securely in the crook of her left arm, Brixia stooped. She was right! Her fingers closed upon the tight bud which had swept over the lake to reveal what lay under its surface. To hold the enfolded blossom once more was comforting. Under the sun it was tightly shut as if it had never opened. Nor did it feel any more as if it pulsed with some life of its own. Brixia tucked it into her shirt, glad of its cool wetness against her skin.

There appeared to be no gate or other opening to lead through the cluster of walls about the two domes. The three splashed their way completely around the outer edge to discover none such. The road they had seen from the bank came to a dead end against one wall. Those partitions arose in a height slightly above Lord Marbon's head, well above Dwed's. Brixia thought she might just be able herself to reach a hand to the top of one while standing on tiptoe.

Marbon was not be baffled. He had made the complete circlet, now he turned to face the nearest stretch of wall. Reaching, he hooked his hands over the top and pulled himself up. He had not spoken since they had come down into the basin of the lake, nor had he shown any sign of realizing he was not alone.

Though the vacancy in his face had gone, his new expression of deep concentration walled them away as completely. he saw only what lay before him—continued with urgency in every movement.

Up and over he went, to drop from sight.

"Lord—!" Dwed must know the futility of such a call as he voiced it. The boy sprang in turn. His first leap fell short so his crooked fingers only drew lines down the still wet surface of the barrier. Before Brixia came up, he jumped again, and this time caught and held, scrambling to the top by a determined effort.

The girl loosened Uta's claw grip on her shoulder and held the cat up. Like it or not Uta would have to take to her own feet now, Brixia could not climb one-handed. And it would seem Uta was willing enough to do just that.

She joined cat and boy on the top of the wall. From here the odd architecture of the building was even more clear. The walls enclosed spaces which jutted out from the double domed center like—like the petals of a flower. They tapered somewhat inward, the space each guarded roughly oval, narrower at the dome end. There was nothing within these enclosures save more water, washing higher here since it had been retained by the walls.

Marbon, water waist high about him, had nearly reached the narrowed end of the space into which he had swung. Now Dwed dropped, heading doggedly after his lord. Brixia hesitated.

Curiosity alone, or so she had thought, had brought her this far. Now, as she crouched on the wall top, she was in two minds about continuing. All the old distrust of sorcery and ancient Powers moved in her. Dwed was drawn by his fierce loyalty to his lord—no such tie moved her. While the alien feeling of the place made her more and more uneasy.

Uta ran lightly along the top of the wall. The cat had

already caught level with Marbon, now passed him, heading for the double-domes. Brixia shook her head. This venture was none of hers. She remained perched where she was, unwilling to go on, yet somehow also unable to go back.

The water washing about on the section below was dim, murky. Anything might swim below its surface. Marbon and Dwed went with their feet and legs covered, she had no such protection. Go back—

But still Brixia could not bring herself to do that. Rather she arose, to balance carefully on the wall top, following Uta's example. The wet surface of the stone was slippery and she advanced slowly, having no desire to slide over.

Lord Marbon reached the far end of the walled enclosure and climbed the wall there. She could see him standing before the nearest of the domes. Uta sprang—not for Marbon's shoulders, but up and out, landing gracefully on the highest point of the dome itself. She leaned over to voice a loud mew as if addressing the man beneath her perch demandingly.

Brixia swayed, fought for her balance. That sound that the cat had made! Her hands flew up to cover her ears. Pain shot through her head like a knife sliding into her flesh. No—!

She could not hear that piercing cry now, she could only feel. While the pain stabs followed near every breath she drew.

There was a mist before her eyes—green-blue. As if the water which had washed here was rising to capture them in a heavy fog of moisture.

"Lord—!"

Dwed's voice—thin—far away—despairing—

The pain stabs came less hard. Brixia strove to see through the mist—

Uta on the dome—Marbon beneath it— The girl uncovered her ears to rub her eyes. She teetered on the wall but made herself edge forward, one fearful step after another. What had happened? That blast of sound—then pain—

Her sight cleared slowly. She could see the dome. See it—and at its crown a dark spot. Uta was gone. Lord Marbon jumped and reached—leaped again, only to slip back. He was striving to gain the place Uta had stood.

Brixia was dizzy, light headed, a little sick. In order to go on she was forced to seat herself on the wall top, hitch along there. Lord Marbon, with a mighty effort, had somehow reached the top of the dome. Then—he was gone! She saw Dwed now leaping vainly to follow, only to slide back again.

"Lord— Lord—!" his voice rang out, but this time the sound of his voice brought no after pain such as had answered Uta's cry.

There was no sight of Marbon or the cat. Brixia reached the end of the wall. Dwed stood against the foot of the dome, his chest heaving. He pounded on the surface before him with his fists. Gingerly Brixia arose to stand upright.

Now she could see more plainly that puzzling alteration in the crest of the dome. There was an opening there! But how to reach it—? She called to Dwed—

"Climb up here. There is a door above there."

He was not long in joining her, still breathing hard from his attempts to scale the dome.

"He's gone—!" Dwed gasped.

Brixia seated herself again, her legs dangling over, hands braced in a tight hold on either side of her body.

"We can't get to him now."

Dwed turned on her fiercely. "Where he went, I will follow!" he said between set teeth.

Let him solve the problem then, Brixia thought. Dwed kicked at her with one foot.

"Move," he ordered. "If I take a run and then jump—"

The girl shrugged. Let him try such tricks. Why she had come this far and involved herself in such madness, she could not understand. She hitched away along the wall, rounding the slightly curved end to allow Dwed room to maneuver.

The boy backed up. Hands on hips, he stood a long moment to measure by eye the wall, the space beyond, the rise of the dome. Then he sat down and pulled off his boots, thrusting their tops under his belt. Feet bare he retreated farther back on the wall.

Turning, he ran, and Brixia watched him, caught in spite of herself in a hope that he would succeed. He leaped out and beyond, his body slamming against the side of the dome. One of his hands caught in the hold he sought, the edge of the opening.

Scrambling against the dome with feet and other hand, he fought until he was able to hook a second hold. Then he drew himself up and disappeared in turn. Brixia sat alone.

Her gaze centered on the dome. Well, they had done it—let the broken-witted lord and his stubborn fosterling seek whatever they believed might lie there. It was none of hers to hunt. Her hands moved restlessly on her knees.

What was Uta's part in all this? That the cat had sought the dome first—had cried out in such a way as to be answered by that frightening sound (or had Uta's cry itself somehow been expanded into that?) Brixia could not deny. But the purpose—?

"Zarsthor's Bane—" she spoke the words aloud. They sounded curiously deadened and far away. Even the water had ceased to wash about the walls and lay almost frighteningly mirror still. And there was a feeling of—of loneliness!

Brixia had long known loneliness. She had endured, come to accept that state as not only safe but natural. But this was a loneliness beyond—beyond what? Once more she was aware of that clarity of sight, that feeling of being claimed by something outside—beyond—

She shook her head, striving to shake loose the grasp of those half feelings—half thoughts—make

them leave her alone. Alone— Brixia gazed up into the arch of the sky. No bird crossed it. This whole valley seemed a deserted, forsaken place. Silence closed about her.

Against her will she gazed once again at the dome—at that opening in the crest which she saw from there only as a shadow against its surface. It—was—none—of—her—desire— She gripped the wall on either side until her fingers were numb with the force she put upon them.

She fought. No—she would not! It—they—*nobody* could make her do this! She would turn—go back—this was no trap of her seeking.

Trap! Memory stirred.

Traps which had beckoned or compelled and which the flower had broken for her. Could the blossom work again? The girl loosened one hand, her fingers stiff, to search within her clothing, to bring the closed bud into the light.

It seemed even more tightly furled now than she remembered it. The flower was dead—it must be—nothing could live this long after being picked.

Brixia raised her hand until the dried looking bud rested just below the level of her chin. There was still a faint scent clinging to it. Somehow sniffing that gave her a shadow of hope.

She breathed deeply once, again— Then lifted her head to gaze to the dome and that opening. She could do as well as Dwed in reaching that, perhaps better. And she was going to! She was not one alone—she was a part of three—

Stowing the bud away again, Brixia got confidently to her feet. As Dwed had done she retreated along the wall, measured the distance with care—ran—and jumped!

Her hands caught on the edge of the opening as they had upon the wall top. Then she heaved up and over. Down into the dark she plunged as one might dive into a lake. But she did not fall far and she landed somehow with a roll she had not consciously planned.

Around her was no complete dark. Rather there shone a blueish gleam which her eyes quickly adjusted to. The chamber was bare, but facing her was a doorway which led in the direction of where the outer tower must stand. Towards that she headed as soon as she regained her feet.

There was a passage beyond opened into another room. Here she found those who had come before her. And—

Brixia gave a cry and dashed forward.

Uta crouched on a pillar her mouth half opened, for between her jaws she held a small box. The hair along the cat's spine stood erect, one forepaw was raised in either threat or warning, while her tail lashed in rage.

Knife in hand Marbon circled the cat, while Dwed crept in on the other side, also with a drawn blade. Uta saw the girl. With one of those leaps such as launched her on prey, she cleared Dwed's shoulder and landed, claws out, against Brixia, ripping the girl's clothing and scratching the flesh beneath as she fought for a more secure hold.

One arm about the cat, her own knife now in hand, Brixia faced the other two. Their expressions chilled her. In the past Marbon had shown a face without life, then one filled with driving eagerness. What looked out of his eyes now was worse than any toad thing's malice. For this emotion dwelt within her own kind— or the likeness of her kind. While Dwed's features had gone slack. He seemed as lacking in consciousness as his lord had earlier been, yet still he moved with cruel purpose. Uta was the quarry for them both.

Brixia backed as Dwed got between her and the door through which she had come. Her shoulders met the wall of the chamber and she slipped along with that at her back even as she had stood at bay before the bird-woman. For some reason they did not rush her. Had they done so they surely could have pulled her down. But, though she was sure they meant to kill her if she did not yield them the cat, they did not yet close in.

The near insane rage in Marbon's eyes spread to twist his features into a mask of cruel purpose. He took a quick step forward. But the result was as if he had tried to walk through the wall itself. Brixia was startled when the man slammed to a full stop, unable to pass some barrier she could not see. Uta's head moved against her. The box was still clamped in the cat's jaws.

But Uta's attention remained fixed on Marbon.

Dwed lingered before the door, knife in hand, guarding that exit, leaving the active hunt to his lord.

Marbon's mouth worked, his lips moved. It he spoke Brixia could hear no sound. Only she felt the cat stiffen against her. Into her own head, burst small thrusts of pain, sharp enough to set her gasping, building up strength with every stab. It was as if some spell the man uttered soundlessly was so translated to her torment.

Around the pillar where Uta had crouched curled a gray mist, wreathing up the length of that as a vine might grow. Marbon continued to attempt to reach at Brixia, pressing first this side and then that. The mist about the pillar towered beyond the crest of that aiming towards the roof of the chamber. There it spread out in long wisps—a shadowy tree putting out branches. Those spread evenly, save directly above the girl and there they did not gather. Whatever protection was about her was present there also.

Uta nudged against her demandingly. The box—did Uta want her to take the box? Brixia reached for it—Uta's head snapped away. What then—?

The cat nosed against the opening of her shirt. Brixia, knife still ready in her hand, pulled open the neck of that. Uta straightway dropped the box within. Now the cat fought against the girl's hold so ruthlessly Brixia dropped her, blood threading along her scratched hands. A moment after landing on the floor, Uta made another spring—she was back again on her pillar perch.

Marbon wheeled. His attention was still for the cat. His lips moved steadily, Brixia now caught a mutter of words.

"Blood to bind, blood to sow, blood to pay. So is it demanded!"

He reached out his left hand and, with his knife, he

scored his own flesh. Without a single wince he waved the wounded hand, flinging a sprinkling of blood drops at the pillar. Dwed walked forward from the door as one walks in a trance.

"Blood to pay—" his lighter, higher voice repeated the words. Now he cut at his hand also and watered the foot of the pillar.

Tendrills of the fog spread out, to fasten on those drops where they had fallen. Brixia could see dark streaks rising from each drop as if the mist drew that into its own substance, fed upon it.

The color of the mist changed. As it darkened it also became more and more opaque. She thought now the illusion was that of stout vines clinging about the pillar, rising to crawl out upon the ceiling. As she raised her eyes, she saw that those were at last moving on over her head, thickening, darkening as they grew. From those stalks above drooped thinner tendrils which swayed, casting back and forth through the air.

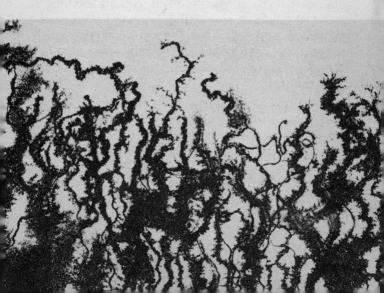

She glanced anxiously at Uta, fearing that the cat might have been already netted by the thicker growth about the pillar. But there was a clear space there within which Uta crouched, snarling.

"We are nothing—but the Power lasts forever!" Marbon cried.

"Fate has written," he continued, "that our kind shall run, has run, beyond all seas. We shall reach earth's last boundaries and shall end as dust shaken from a traveler's boot. But ahead in the heavens still lies Power, and those there are the Lords of outer space!"

There were powers and powers, Brixia thought wildly. What gathered here gave off a stench, ever thickening as the evil tree thing took on substance. The same noisome smell she had met with the toad things and the birds filled her nostrils. Her knife fell from her hand. Its too often sharpend blade shattered against the stone floor. But she did not heed those splinters of metal. Rather she groped for the bud dead and brown. When she held that safe within her hand she became only a door, a mouth—a way for another presence to enter her world. It was true, at least she knew what part she had in this—she was a servant and now full service was demanded of her.

10

BRIXIA MOISTENED her lips with tongue tip. She felt strange—as if there was now a veil between her and the past— Who or what invaded her now, used her for a mouthpiece—or a tool? Whatever force of personality possessed her (and she could not detect the nature of the compulsion present in control) it was not born of her own will, thought, or being.

"Hatred does not last forever, no matter how hot or how deep it has run," that other will brought the words out of her now. "If those who gave it birth are gone it dwindles and dies. But in the brilliant light of the past may lie the seeds of future glory—for those secrets rest hidden in the minds of man." So did that presence give tongue.

Marbon stared at her. Once more he appeared fully awake, conscious, the man he once had been, might again be, coming into part life once more. This vigor which blazed up in him centered in his eyes. Those appeared cored by a ruddy spark of hunger. Brixia felt as if his demanding gaze dug and pried at her, as one

155

might strive to hunt from its safe protection some shell dwelling creature.

"That was the thoughts of Jartar!" He hissed the name. "I know not how or why I can swear this! But Jartar—" his voice died away, there was a flush across his high cheekbones.

That which possessed Brixia spoke again. Her voice sounded different in her own ears, deeper, harsher.

"Hate dies—but while it lives it can twist and torment the unwary who summon its aid. However old the hates—even those backed by a Power can lose their strength—"

"Lord!"

Dwed's cry, one of amazement and fear, cut across her speech. The boy had come a step or two forward from the doorway. He was no longer blank of face, rather seemed one who was but an extension of a stronger will.

Around his body twined a dark tendril loosed from the vine of mist. He struggled to throw that off, slashing furiously at it with his free hand. To no purpose, for the mist, which seemed more and more a tangible thing, clung and could not be loosened.

His face was stricken with fear as he writhed more and more vigorously against the whispy stuff. But thin as it looked it appeared well able to keep him in thrall.

"Lord!" his repeated cry was a frantic plea.

Marbon did not even turn his head to glance at his fosterling. Rather his gaze centered and narrowed upon Brixia, even as a man about to match sword against sword watches his enemy.

"Eldron, if you are here to protect the Bane," he challenged sharply, "then I am also! I am of Zarsthor's line—ours the ancient quarrel—if you do not sulk within your Power—then show yourself!"

"Lord!" The mist arose farther about Dwed. He was enwrapped by it save for his white and stricken face, now a mask of fear. "Lord, by your powers—save me!"

That which was still Brixia, not entirely possessed by the entity which made use of her as a vessel for other thought and emotions (Jartar's or Eldor's, who could tell) knew what held Dwed was surely beyond the boy's strength to resist. That his courage had already so broken before the lord he worshipped must seem to him black defeat.

"The Bane!" Still Marbon gave no heed to his fosterling.

He strode to advance upon the girl, beat with his hand in rage against that invisible barrier between them. He even slashed the air with his knife as if he could tear that asunder as he might fabric tight stretched.

"Give me the Bane!" he shouted.

Now about his feet the mist tendrils gathered in turn, puddled and thickened. The fog drew about him, crept upward along his body. It lapped his knees, clung to his thighs but he did not seem to notice.

Only Dwed hung in the stuff as a spider's prey is enwrapped in web, helpless, motionless. The horror on his face was stark as wavelets of the mist touched his cheeks, clung to his chin.

"The Bane!" Marbon mouthed.

Uta stood tall on her hind feet. She slapped out viciously at a tongue of the mist reaching for her. At that same moment Brixia was—emptied. She had no other word to describe that sensation of release. Something had withdrawn. She was now alone, open to whatever Marbon might use against her. Even her knife lay shattered at her feet.

Her hand closed convulsively as if she could still grip the haft of that weapon. But what she held was the bud. And it moved! As her fingers spread flat, the flower began to open.

The dull brown outer husks split. From the heart within came that glow which had lightened her path, heartened her, during her journey through the night in the Waste.

Powers and powers, she thought frantically. Now her other hand went to that box Uta had entrusted to her, closed on it where it lay within her shirt.

Marbon stirred. His face was no longer that of the man she knew—slack or conscious either one. Could it be possible that features *could* writhe in that intolerable fashion—resettle into an entirely different countenance? Even if this change was only illusion, it was surely never meant for any one sane to witness. She was icy cold, now filled with such terror that she could not will herself to the slightest movement towards escape, even though Dwed now left the door open for her going.

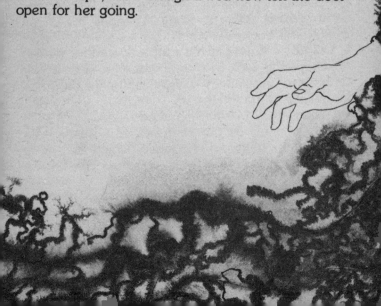

The man fronting her flung high his arms. His face turned up to the twining, squirming snakes of fog above them. He called:

"Jartar—sle—frawa—ti!"

The mist whirled in a pattern which made one dizzy to watch. Brixia, now that Marbon's gaze no longer held and commanded hers, closed her eyes lest she lose her senses watching the vortex of the fog. Then the fragrance of the flower wafted upward to clear her head.

What he might have called on she could not guess. But—something answered. It was here—with her— for, though she did not open her eyes to look, she was sure this new presence loomed near her—reached out—

Box and flower—she did not know why the two came together in her mind and that combination seemed right—needful. Flower and box—Do not look! What is here had come to cloud her thoughts, lessen what she might do to defend herself. There was a tugging which she must not yield to.

Once more the cry arose from her, the appeal to the only thing which seemed to promise safety in this shifting and alien world.

"Green mother, what must I do? This is no magic of my own—in these ways am I lost!"

Did she in truth cry that aloud, or was it only thought so intense that it seemed open speech, a plea made perhaps fruitlessly to a power she could not understand? Who were the gods—those great sources of power who were reputed to use men and women as tools and weapons? And did those so used have any defenses at all? Was this struggle now centering on her as battle between one alien power and another?

Open!

An order—delivered by whom—or what? The thing Marbon had summoned? If so she was indeed in danger. Brixia still kept her eyes tightly closed, tried to do the same for her mind. As the mist had made a prisoner of Dwed, so did the will she sensed strive to enmesh her—not in body but in mind.

"By what I hold," Brixia cried aloud, "let me stand fast!"

Box and flower—

Her hands moved, bringing together the two objects she held. She could not be sure whether she acted by the commands of the Light, or the Dark. But it was done. And at the same moment she opened her eyes.

There was—

She was not in the mist curtained room of the pillar, rather she stood before the high seat in the feast hall of a keep. There were torches blazing high in the rings fastened to the stone of the walls. A cloth woven of many colors, each hue fading or deepening into the next, lay down the center of the board. And on that cloth were drinking horns of gleaming crystal, of the rich green of malachite, the warm red-brown of carnelian, such a display as only the greatest of the dale lords might hope to equal.

Before each place was a platter of silver. And there were many dishes and bowls set out—some bearing patterned edges, or set with the wink of gems.

At first Brixia thought that she stood in a deserted

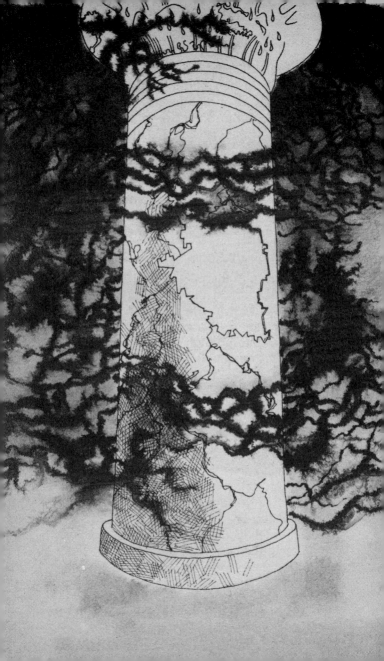

hall and then she discovered that there was indeed a company there, but those who sat to feast were but the faintest of shadows, mere wisps so tenuous that she could not be sure which was man and which woman. It was as if that which was inert could be clearly seen, but life to her eyes was that of those shades which some dalespeople said clung to old, ill-omened places and were inimical to the living out of jealousy and despair at their own unhappy state.

Brixia cried out. She swayed, fought to move from where she stood directly before the high seat where he or she who ruled this shadow company might mark her presence in a moment. But she could not flee, no, she was fast held to face what might come.

A black flash—if light *could* be dark instead of white, slashed between her and the high seat, as a sword might swing to set a barrier of moving steel. Crooked and controlled, a will which was not wholly evil, yet carried with it the stigmata of the dark, was like a blow as it strove to seize upon her. It flailed at her like a harshly laid on lash. And now it seemed that the ghost shape in the high seat did indeed turn upon her visible eyes of red flame.

The shadow deepened even as Marbon's features had appeared to move and change, grew to be more substance. It seemed to the girl that what crouched now in that high backed chair was no noble lord such as might rule this hall. Rather that which leered at her with those flame eyes, which might have been wrought from the coals of hell itself, was an outlaw, foul, the very worst of the brutes she had in the past fled, or hidden from, knowing well what would happen to her were she to fall into their hands.

Gone!

Crouched on the high seat now was a toad thing from the Waste—obscenely bloated, its toothed jaws agape, its clawed paws outstretched. A giant among its

kind, fully as large and menacing as the outlaw shape it
had replaced. It gabbled in distorted speech:

"Bane—the Bane!"

Box and flower—

Brixia came aware that she was pressing both of
these with bruising force against her breast. Box and
flower—

The toad thing winked out. Now it was the bird-
woman. Her cruel bill clicked, she held high her arm
wings, the talons crooked, and it would seem she was
on the very point of hurling herself into the air, launch-
ing an attack on Brixia.

Illusions? The girl could not be sure. For as each
appeared it was as solid, seemingly as substantial as
the seat in which it sat or squatted. Box and flower—

Now—now it was Dwed! Still enwrapped in the mist
he lay limply rather than sat in the high seat. All was
hidden save a portion of his face. He raised his head
weakly, looked at her with eyes which were dulled
with horror and yet held in them a desperate plea:

"Bane—" The single word was a tortured whisper
which echoed hollowly all through that hall.

Then—he was gone. In his place Uta—Uta firmly
visible but in the grip of a monster shadow thing,
twisting, fighting vainly to free herself ever as the mis-
shapen paws netted tight about her furred throat to
squeeze all life from her.

"Bane!" the cat squawked.

As had the others Uta vanished. For a long moment
the high seat seemed empty. Then—no more
shadow—here was a man as visible and as real as
Marbon had been when he fronted her in the bubble
room.

He wore mail, not the silken robe of a feaster, and a
helmet overshadowed his face.

"Marbon!" Brixia near spoke that name aloud and
then she saw that this was not the stricken Lord of

Eggarsdale, though there was surely some close kin line linking them one to the other. But on this man's face a harsh and arrogant pride had set an unbreakable seal. And there was a twist about his lips as if he bit upon something sour and unpalatable which poisoned any pleasure of this feasting.

Like their lord the others ranged there became the clearer. Nor were they all, Brixia realized with a shiver, of the human kind. There was a lady robed in the green of new spring leaves who sat upon the right hand of the lord. But her flowing hair was as delicately and freshly green as the gown which she wore, and her face, beautiful as it was, was not that of a human woman. On the other seat, to the lord's left, a cat's head arose not so far above the level of the table. In color it might have been Uta but Brixia believed, could she see it better, this strange feline would have been half again as large.

There were others—a young man wearing a helm on which the crest was a rearing horse, and whose face had an unhuman cast—not as pronounced as that of the green woman, but unmistakable. There was another woman plainly robed in cloth the color of steel, girdled with metal plates each of which was centered by a milk-white gem. Her hair, as white as those gems, was braided about her head so that it itself formed a crown of presence. And her calm face held strength and assurance. Yet there was about her some of the feeling that she was apart from this company, an onlooker at what might pass here, and yet not a partaker in any action. On her breast rested an intricately fashioned pendant of the same white stones. And Brixia felt that served its owner for as powerful a weapon as any war blade.

At the far end of the table, where the other feasters appeared to have withdrawn a little to give them room (as if they were not entirely welcome), were two others. Brixia, seeing them clearly, caught her breath.

That grotesque and attenuated creature who had been served by birds— This was not quite her double. The half female figure was more rounded, closer to that of a woman, though unclothed save for the feathers. Also the avian creature wore a gemmed belt. While more jewels sparked from a wide collar-like necklace. But that she was of the same breed as the Waste creature there could be no doubt.

Next to her squatted one of the Toads—save there was a closer, near blasphemous link between this monstrosity and—a man? Brixia loathed the thought, yet she could not escape it as her gaze, in spite of all her efforts, were drawn to the creature.

Its eyes glittered with malice and she could guess that, though it appeared to be here in acceptance if not in friendship, it liked its present company no more than the company welcomed it.

It would seem that Brixia's own presence aroused no interest in the feasters. Not one pair of eyes sought her out in surprise, nor even appeared to rest on her long enough to recognize that she was not truly of them. What purpose had brought her here she did not understand. Then—

She no longer stood helplessly fixed before the high seat. After a moment of startlement she realized that she now, by some feat of power (or the will of that which had sent her here) appeared to hang in the air above the feasters, in a manner which enlarged her view of the whole hall and those in it.

The high chair of the lord faced, as was still the dales custom in any keep of pretension, the great double outer door of the hall itself. Now, with a crash which brought instant silence to the mumurs which Brixia had been able to hear only as a faint sighing of sound, that portal not only burst open, but the two leaves were sent flying back to slam against the wall. It was as

if a thunder clap had been wrested out of some summer storm to resound through the hall.

Within the cavernous opening of the door (for that portal might well have admitted without difficulty near a full company of fighting men in marching order) there stood a single man. As the lord of the hall he was not dressed for feasting, but also wore mail and a helmet. While thrown back on his shoulders was a cloak lying in folds as if he had tossed it so impatiently to free his arms for some meeting of swords.

Yet the blade which he wore was still in its scabbard and he held no weapon. No weapon save the hate which was naked in his face. And Brixia who had near called "Marbon" upon her first sighting of the hall lord, was now almost convinced that she would make no mistake in giving that name in truth to this newcomer.

He did not advance at once into the hall but waited, as if he must have some invitaton, or at least recognition, from the man in the high seat. While he so stood quietly, surveying the company at large, there was an ingathering of followers behind him.

It was if he were a man standing amid a company of children. For these who stepped forward to flank him, massed in place at his back, were of the size to make him seem a giant. Yet they had the seeming, not of the children whose size they aped, rather of being well matured and perhaps even of some unusual age.

They did not have the stocky bodies of dwarves, but were slender and well shaped. Only their small hands, their finely featured faces, were uncovered. For the rest they wore a mail which had the pearling of the interior of a shell, made in small plates which overlapped. While their helmets were unmistakably either giant shells, or else faithfully fashioned in that pattern.

"Greeting, kinsman—"

It was the lord of the hall who broke the uneasy

silence that had fallen upon the echoing of the door crash. He was smiling a little, but it was an unpleasant smile with a gloating in the curve of his lips.

The man at the door met him eye to eye. He wore no smile, rather there was that in faint lines about his nostrils and his lips which said that only with great effort did he hold his emotions under tight rein. Nor did he come any farther into the hall.

"You did not signify that you intended to honor us with your presence," continued the lord. "But there is always room for a kinsman in Kathal—"

"Such room as is in An-Yak?" for the first time the newcomer spoke. His voice was low but Brixia had an odd sense that she could feel within herself the strain he was under to keep his rage in bonds.

"A strange question, kinsman. What may you mean by it? Have you and your water people then some trouble lying upon you?"

The man at the door laughed. "A proper question, Eldor! Trouble you ask? And why must you ask that? Surely with your eyes and ears, your readers of the wind, and listeners to the grass, the birds, all else able to bear rumor or report the truth, you already know what has happened."

The lord shook his head. "You credit me with many powers, Lord Zarsthor. Had I but a fraction of such I need question no man—"

"Then why do so?" snapped Zarsthor. "Trouble—yes, we know trouble. It is the kind which comes from ill wishing, from the meddling with forces which darken a man to touch upon. I have not such great reach as you can muster, Eldor, still have I heard of certain Callings, of bargains, and trysts, and stirrings in strange place. They speak to me of a Bane—"

Another silence fell as he said that last word—such a silence as was more potent than a battle cry shouted aloud. There was not even a stir among the company. They might have been frozen, each one, into instant and lasting immobility.

It was the woman of the white gems who broke that silence.

"You speak in anger, Lord Zarsthor—a hasty speech cannot be recalled for even one word."

For the first time his eyes flickered away from Eldor, touched upon the woman, and were instantly back upon the lord, as if he needed to keep him ever in sight for a very necessary reason of his own. He spoke respectfully but he did not look at her again as he so answered:

"Your grace, I am angry, yes. But a man can be angered by truth and so armored against injustice, and creeping evil. My friends have also certain powers. There has been a Bane laid upon me, upon An-Yak—I am willing to swear this on oath at your very altar, under the fullness of your moon!"

Now the woman turned her head and looked directly at Eldor.

"It has been said that there is a Bane raised against a lord and his land. To this there must be an answer—"

Eldor's smile grew wider. "Do not trouble yourself, your grace. Is it not true that what lies between kinsman and kinsman are private things, resting alone on them?"

Now it was the youth wearing the horse-topped helm who broke in. Under the shadow of his elaborate helmet his dark brows drew close in a deep frown.

"Between kin and kin no one but a sworn liegeman may raise his voice, such is in truth the custom, Lord Eldor. But a Bane is not such a light thing as to be used without due consideration. I have been asking myself since we gathered here why certain ones have been honored among us for the first time." He nodded and that inclination of his head clearly indicated both the toad creature and the avian woman at the other end of the table.

Now there was a low murmur, which seemed to Brixia to be mainly one of assent, spreading from one to the next among the other guests. Yet neither the bird-woman nor the Toad—if their features could indeed register any real emotion—seemed to show either surprise or irritation at being so singled out.

The green haired lady's voice, as light and delicate as a breeze rustling among river reeds, followed fast upon that spreading murmur:

"Lord Eldor, unmeet as it is for guests to make such comments, yet so is this land now arrayed, one power fronting against the next, that it might be wise for you to forget the lack of proper courtesy and answer—"

11

"WELL DO YOU SAY, Lady Lalana, it is not courtesy to question the arrangements of your host at a feasting. But since this is now a matter of openness in our company—why, I do not stand under any shadow with a need for hiding what I have done, or will do." His confidence was high with arrogance at that moment.

"It is true that there is a separation among us of Arvon and this grows the wider—mainly because no one raises a voice to ask why does this happen? We are not of one blood or one kind, yet for long we have managed to dwell peaceably side by side—"

The woman of the white gems arose. Her calm face was in a manner, Brixia sensed, a rebuke to the speaker. Her hand came up breast high between them and her fingers moved in a gesture which the watching girl was not able to follow. But what was a marvel was that those movements left drawn on the air itself a symbol as if white fire, not springing from any tangible source, blazed there.

For a moment out of time that symbol stayed

white—as pure as the light of the full summer moon. Then it began to shade as if blood itself seeped in from an unknown space to taint and corrupt it. From a flushing of pink it turned ever darker, though still its outlines remained intact and sharp to the eye.

Full crimson it became. But the change was not yet over—darker and darker—now it held a blackness which at last was entire— Then the symbol itself began to writhe in the air, as if the change brought about some weird torment to substances which lived and could suffer pain.

So at last the white symbol was now a black one and its whole character was changed. While those around the feast board stared at it with grave faces which grew even more disturbed and uneasy. Only the avian woman and the toad creature seemed utterly undisturbed and unimpressed.

Even Eldor took a step backward. Now his own hand half lifted as if he would reach out to erase from sight that sullenly glowing stain upon the air of the hall. But his fist fell back to his side again. However his face was stern set with purpose.

It was not he, however, who broke the silence in which all those within the hall seemed to be holding their breath waiting for some catastrophic event. Rather the woman who had drawn the symbol spoke:

"So be it—" Her three words rang out as might judgment in some court whose pronouncement could alter the fate of whole nations.

Apparently in answer to those words the major part of that company arose from their places, turning to Eldor faces which were set and accusing. But he held his head high and gazed back with a defiance as protective as the armor he wore.

"I am lord in Varr." He also spoke with emphasis as if the words had a double meaning.

The woman of the white gems inclined her head a fraction.

"You are lord in Varr," she agreed in a neutral voice. "Thus do you affirm your lordship. But also must a lord answer for that land of which he is warden—in the end."

He showed teeth in a wolfish grin. "Yes, lordship is a burden to be accounted for. Do not think, your grace, that I did not consider that before—"

"Before you wrought with them!" Zarsthor came a few steps farther into the hall. His arm was raised as if he would hurl the spear he did not hold, the index finger of his hand pointing to toad and bird-woman.

Eldor snarled. "I said I would settle with you, kinsman! You laid shame on me, now worse shall lay on you and your land, and those fish men with whom you lair! Eaters of filth, dwellers in mud, profaners of the world—" his voice arose into near a shout. "You have spit upon the name of your House and brought our blood near to the dust—"

As Eldor's rage showed the hotter, Zarsthor's expression became one of emotionless calm. The warriors in scaled armor who had followed him into the hall drew closer about him. Their sword hands hung now close to the hilts of their scabbarded weapons and Brixia saw them glancing swiftly right and left as if they expected to have enemies leap forward from the walls of the chamber.

"Ask of yourself, Eldor," Zarsthor spoke as the other paused for breath, "with whom *you* have consorted. What price have *you* paid for the Bane? To surrender Varr perhaps—"

"Ahhhh—" his answer was a howl of pure rage. But a movement at the far end of the table drew Brixia's attention, as small as that shifting of position had been.

The avian woman held up her goblet, was looking down into the cup with intense concentration. What she saw there might be of far more interest to her at this moment than the exchange before the two lords. Her head bent forward in a sudden bob. Had her vile mouth dipped into the liquid, or had she, on the contrary, spat into it? Brixia could not tell. But moving with almost a blur of speed she now hurled the cup from her directly into the center of the table before Eldor's high seat.

There was a flash of—could flame be *black*?—which flared up as the goblet smashed against the board and spattered its contents outward. There were cries. People reeled back and away from the outward curling black flames which continued to blaze.

Even Eldor staggered in retreat, his arm flung up before his face to protect himself. While those others, the green lady, the rest, fled as the fire licked out viciously as if to lash them.

Darker grew the flames and higher. They blotted out the scene for Brixia. She caught a glimpse of some of the company in flight through the door, Zarsthor and his shell-helmed followers mixed with them.

At the same time she was aware that the box she held in her hand—that which Uta had given her—was warm—no,, hot—until the heat grew close to torment. Still she could not loose her hold and drop it.

The hall was gone—with it the black fire. The girl was caught in a place of gray nothingness. She found herself breathing in great gasps as if there were little air here and she could not find enough to fill her laboring lungs.

Then the grayness became a stretch of ground—barren—rift by furrows—but not the furrows set by any landman's plow. No, this was as if some great sword had hacked and hacked again—its cutting blade driving all vestiges of life out of the wastage of leached earth.

Farther the mist lifted to show more and more of the

gray and ravaged land. Yet Brixia knew by some means that this had once been a fair country before the shadow had fallen on it. She saw tumbled blocks, stained by time, and with the faint shadows of fire scorch laid across them, and believed that once there had stood here some great keep, proud and fine.

Now—out of the curtain of mist which had withdrawn only a short way—there came from either side—two men. About them hung a visible cloud which the girl realized was the hate which corroded and ate at them until they had naught else to keep them living. Though this place was not of their world, (How did she know that also, Brixia wondered fleetingly) rather a hell that they had made for themselves through time itself. No matter who had had the right of it when this had begun, both now were tainted, defiled by the war which had held them, turning in desperation and rage to the Dark when the Light would not support them. Now they were entrapped—always to wander in their hell.

Their mail was hacked, rusted with blood. Though they still wore sword belts, neither had a blade. Only their hatred remained as their weapon.

Now one raised a hand and hurled a ball of force of rage and hate at his adversary. That broke against the other's breastplate in a rain of dark sparks. He reeled back a step or two, but did not fall.

Instead he who had been struck clapped his hands together. There followed no sound. But the man who had thrown the ball shook from head to foot as might a young tree in the full blast of a winter storm.

Brixia, without any volition on her part, against her will, moved forward until she stood halfway between the two of them. Their heads came slowly around so she could see their faces in the shadow of their battered helms. Their features were withered, scored by

passion, yet she knew them for Eldor and Zarsthor—old in hate.

Each held forth a hand, not imploringly, but in command. They spoke together so that it sounded to her like a single sharp order:

"Bane!"

Nor did they after fade as had the others—the outlaw, the toad—Uta— Rather their figures looked even clearer, in a way brighter. Eldor spoke again when she did not move:

"Give it to me, I say! It is mine, I labored in its making, I made a pact with those I distrusted, I gave much to have it! If you will not yield it willingly, then I shall *call* and what will come to my aid will serve you as you choose—for the choice is yours!"

Zasthor spoke as urgently:

"It is mine! Since it was wrought to break me, and all those who stood with me, then by the very right of Power, I have now the need to defeat it, and him—give him back from my own hand that which he raised to damn me. I must have it!"

In Brixia's hand the box glowed warm. And in her other hand lay the flower. It seemed to her oddly that each weighed much, but the weight was the same, and in her way she was a balance appointed to hold them so. This was in manner a judgment she did not understand, to be delivered to those whose causes she could not know. One had threatened her—Eldor. Zarsthor's words might have been taken as a justification and a plea.

"I wrought it!"

"I fought it!"

That they cried together.

"Why?" Her question seemed to startle both of them. How could she hope to render judgment when she knew so little of the rights of the matter which had brought them at each other's throats?

For a moment they were silent. Then Eldor moved a step closer, both his hands out as if to take the box from her by force if he must.

"You have no choice," he told her fiercely, "what I shall summon shall surely answer. And that coming shall be *your* bane!"

"Give it to him if you are fearful! But you will never then know how empty his threats may be," Zarsthor broke in. "Give it to him, thereafter you shall walk in the shadow of fear for as long as you live—and even after! Even as we two now must walk in this place because of the Bane."

Box and flower—

Brixia found she could break the gaze with which they had held her, their eyes keeping her prisoner. Now she looked down at her two hands—at what those held in balance.

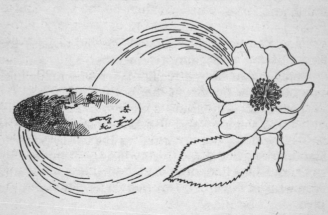

The box was open! Tight held within it lay an oval stone—light pulsed weakly from its visible surface. That light was gray, like a film of shadow—if shadow and light could be one. The flower had also opened to its greatest extent and the light which came from it was not the pure white which she had always before seen, but rather a green glow which was soft and soothing to her eyes.

"This is the Bane, then," she said slowly. "Why was it wrought, Eldor—truly—why?"

His face was grim and hard.

"Because I would deal with my enemy as I must—" .

"No," Brixia shook her head. "Not as you must—but rather as you chose, is that not so? And why was he your enemy—?"

The harsh face grew even sterner. "Why? Because—because—" His voice trailed away, she saw him bite upon his lower lip.

"Is it that you no longer know?" the girl asked as he continued to hestiate.

He frowned at her fiercely but he did not answer. She turned to Zarsthor.

"Why did he so hate you that he had to make this evil thing?"

"I—I—"

"You also no longer know." She did not ask this time. "But if you cannot remember why you are enemies—what does it really matter who holds this? You no longer need it, is that not the truth?"

"I am Eldor—the Bane is mine to use as I see fit!"

"I am Zarsthor—and the Bane has brought me this—" he flung out his arms, his hands clasped into fists, to indicate the ravaged world about them.

"I am Brixia," the girl said, "and—I am not sure what else at this time. But that which abides in me says—let it be thus!"

She brought the flower above the box, made the dim light of that greenish glow fall upon the gray stone within.

"Power of destruction—power of growth and life. Let us now see which is master—even here!"

The gray film on the stone no longer appeared to move. Rather it lay like a still crust over the surface.

And, as the light continued to bathe that crust, it broke, flaked away to reveal new radiance. While the flower slowly dimmed, its petals drew in, began to wither. Brixia wanted to jerk it away from that devouring stone, but her hand would not obey. More and more the flower shriveled, the stone in turn glowed and pulsed. It was no longer the gray of death—of this land which was a trap—rather it now had a green spark at its heart, it could have been a seed ready to break through its protective casing and put forth new life.

Of the flower all which was left was a wisp, a frail skeleton of a blossom. Then there was nothing at all. Her hand was bare. But in her other palm the box was also crumbling, loosing its hold on the stone. Bit by bit it powdered away into dust.

There was no longer any warmth in the stone. If any energy dwelt within it, that was more isolated than had been the Power in the flower. But its beauty was such that Brixia was awed by what she held. Then she looked beyond it from Eldor to Zarsthor.

She held the stone out towards Eldor.

"Do you wish this now? I think it is no longer what you once wrought, but would you have it?"

The frown had been smoothed from his face and with it many of the hard lines which had aged and ravaged it. Dignity was still there and authority but behind those emotions—a freedom. His eyes were alight, but he snatched back his hand hurriedly as hers, holding the stone, approached the closer.

"This I did not make. No Power granted me fills it. I can no longer demand it by right for my own."

"And you?" Brixia offered it now to Zarsthor.

He gazed at the stone absorbedly, not looking to her. Then, without raising his eyes, he answered:

"That which was meant to be my Bane—no, this is not it. Green magic is life, not death. Though death has brought to me through that as it was once. But I cannot break this as I would have the Bane—loosed its evil upon all. This is yours, lady, do with it as you will. For—" he raised his head and looked about him, there was peace in his face, underlying a great weariness. "The geas which bound us in this world of our own making is broken. It is time we take our rest."

Together they turned away from Brixia, Zarsthor moved up beside Eldor shoulder to shoulder. As if they had long been shield brothers and not deadly enemies, they marched on, following some road only they could see, into the mist.

Brixia cradled the stone in her two hands. As if she awakened from some absorbing dream she looked about her with the beginning of new uneasiness.

That this place was not of any time or world she had known she was sure. How might she now return to her own place? Or could she? Panic began to grow from the seed of that first uneasiness. She called loudly:

"Uta! Dwed!" And finally—"Marbon!"

Then she listened, hoping against all hope that there would be an answer to guide her. A second time she shouted, this time more loudly—only to hear nothing when her own voice died away.

Names—as all knew names had a power of their own—they were a part of one—as much as skin, hair, or teeth. They were given to one at the birth hour and were thereafter something which could be threatened by evil, used to strengthen good. Now all she had to aid her were names. Still two of those she called upon had no ties with her, nor perhaps held any wish to aid, and the third was an animal, alien to her own kind. Perhaps she had no ties to draw her back at all.

Brixia lifted her cupped hands, stared at the stone. This was truly a thing of Power. It had been wrought to bring evil, even as Eldor (or the part of him who had existed here) had claimed and Zarsthor in turn had agreed. But its evil had somehow been discharged by the flower. Could it serve her, she who had no command over any force, no training as a Wise Woman?

"Uta"—this time she did not shout that name aloud into the mist, rather spoke it softly to the stone. "Uta, if you have any fair feeling for me now—if I am granted any desire of yours for my salvation—Uta—where are you?"

The light glow began to pulse in ripples from the stone. A deeper green sparked in its heart—grew and spread. Brixia strove to keep her thoughts fixed on Uta.

That dark spot put out pricked ears, opened slits of eyes, became a head. The head in turn pushed out of

the surface of the stone. Brixia, almost beyond wonder now, crouched down, held her hand closer to the earth. The tiny image of the cat was three dimensional as it arose from the stone. When it was fully clear it leaped to the ground.

Mist which had been encroaching ever since Eldor and Zarsthor had gone, curled back from where the cat stood. Uta's image turned its head up to the girl, its tiny mouth opened. But if it mewed she caught no sound. Then it began to trot away and Brixia scrambled to follow it.

The fog swirled in, covering her own body to knee level. But it did not hide the cat, a clear space continued to encircle and move with it. She hurried to catch up as the illusion—if that was what it was—moved faster.

How far they had come across the hidden land Brixia could not tell. Then her guide slowed, and, to her despair, began to fade.

"Uta!" She screamed. She could see through the small body now—it was fast becoming a part of the mist.

Brixia went to her knees. Without Uta she was lost—and now Uta was nearly gone. Only an outline in the fog remained. If she could only bring it back! Now— Uta had come when she called her name and concentrated on the stone—but perhaps the cat's powers were not strong enough to hold her here until her mission could be accomplished.

What of Marbon—Dwed? The man might be counted her enemy—at least he had seemed so before she had been caught into this place. While the boy then had been entrapped in enchantment. Even if she could reach them—dared she hope for any help?

Dwed—Marbon—which should she try?

The man had been free when last she saw him—

except for the obsession which had ridden him. Brixia raised the stone to eye level.

"Marbon!" she summoned.

There was no darkening of the stone heart, nor any sign that her call had reached him, whether or not he would answer her plea.

"Marbon!" Because she thought it now her only hope she called again.

A rippling in the stone, yes, but faint and with nothing centered in it. However, as she dropped her hand in despair, she saw Uta a little beyond her again!

From and clear, larger—seemingly substantial, Uta was watching her impatiently, her mouth opening and closing in soundless mews. Brixia jumped to her feet, ready to follow. Had Marbon in some way strengthened the cat? She did not know—but that Uta was here again gave her a lighter heart.

Uta began to run and Brixia after her. The sense of urgency spread from cat to girl. On—

Then a huge, dark pillar loomed out of the mist, rising so suddenly that Brixia felt it had not been there long, but rather risen abruptly to front her. Uta stood on hind legs, pawed with her forefeet at its surface, plainly urging on the girl the need to climb.

She tucked the stone within her shirt once more for safe keeping, then she sought on the pillar some holds for fingers and toes. Uta—vanished. She had not faded slowly as before, but simply winked out.

Brixia found by touch irregularities in the pillar her eyes could not detect. With effort she began to climb. The holds were small and the higher she went the slower her progress became. Yet she was winning upward, if it were only a matter of a few fingers length at a time.

Up and up, she knew better than to look down. Her fingers ached and then grew numb. Her whole body was tense as it pressed against the pillars. Fear was a heavy burden resting on her. Up and still up—

How long had she climbed? There was no counting of time in this place—moments might have spun out into days—perhaps months. Always above her the pillar reached higher still and there were hanging drapes of mist to hide its crest—if it *had* a crest!

Brixia felt as if she could not seek another hand hold, the pain in her shoulders was intense. Up—ever up! She could not lift her hand again, the effort was too great. Soon her grip would break and she would fall—back—to be swallowed up in the mist and forever lost.

"Uta!" her voice was a croaked whisper which she had no hope would be answered.

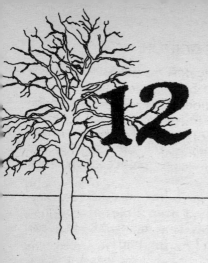

12

OUT OF THE MIST cloaking what lay above her there reached— A giant paw! The claws were unsheathed, extended in threatening curves just above her as that paw swung down in menace. Brixia clung despairingly to the pillar. But her hold was not tight enough. The claws hooked into her shirt over the shoulders and she was torn loose from her precarious grasp on the shaft, brought up through the mist ceiling. Up—and down—for she was released and fell, scraping her arm against stone, a wild yowl ringing in her ears.

The pillar was still by her. But this was not the pillar she had climbed—this was small—she could span it with her outflung arm. It formed a pedestal on the crown of which crouched Uta—a normal sized Uta— The cat stared down and Brixia realized she was back in her own time and space.

This was the same chamber in the once drowned building of the lake. But there was no mist-vine choking walls and ceiling now. Those walls, blue-green and gleaming, were as bright as if newly scoured. On the floor, just a little beyond where she was crouched, lay

Dwed, his head and shoulders supported by Lord Marbon!

There was no slackness in Marbon's face as he gazed distractedly at her over the boy's body. Nor was he under the hold of any power now. She sensed he was truly human, with his own mind unlocked to free him from the shadow as well as the obsession which had imprisoned him.

"Dwed—dies—" He gave her no other greeting, nor did he act as if he had been a part of what had happened to her. His eyes were haunted by fear, not for himself she knew, but for the boy.

What he said might be true—but she was not willing to accept such a despairing judgment. Brixia did not get to her feet, rather she crept closer on her hands and knees. That vast fatigue which had settled on her during her climb out of that other place still weighed her body. Reaching the two she fumbled in her shirt and brought out the stone.

"This is a thing of power," she said slowly. "I do not know how to use it—but when I called with it—Uta answered. I called upon you also—did you then hear?"

He frowned. "I had—it was a dream—I think."

"No dream." Her hands shook as she cupped the stone. "Perhaps—perhaps—if Dwed has not gone too far, him also we can call. Look upon this, lord, and call your fosterling!" Her words had the sharpness of an order as she thrust the stone into his full view, holding it directly above Dwed's body.

As if she had left him no choice Marbon's intent gaze dropped to the stone. Animation was once more gone from his features, his face appeared drawn and wasted—near as old as had been the countenance of Zarsthor in that other world. He, too, might have fought some age long battle of mind and spirit—his eyes alone seemed alive.

Brixia hesitated. Dwed had no friend or liege tie with her. Would a call shaped by her thought reach him, be strong enough to halt his march into those shadows which enclosed the Last Gate of all? But if Marbon did such calling, could she not in turn fortify him in some way—her will alone perhaps giving him additional strength?

"Call!" she ordered once more. At the same time she summoned all she knew of concentration and aimed her will, not at the motionless, scarcely breathing body, but into the heart of the stone she held now near touching his breast.

"Call Dwed!"

Perhaps Marbon did—silently. Was it the stone which drew Brixia then into a state of being which no voice might reach? She—or a part of her holding her strong will and innermost spirit—was engulfed, swept on—not back into that place of mists from which she had brought the altered Bane. No, this was darker, more threatening, cold, dreary—a place of despair.

"Dwed!" Now she herself shaped that name in her thought, not with her lips. And it seemed to her the soundless thought rang like an imperative shout.

Down— Brixia had a sensation of sinking further and further into this dead world. There was a swirl of dusky green light about her but it did nothing to make her less apprehensive.

"Dwed!" Not *her* thought-call this time. But when she caught it she hastened to echo it. Before her stretched a line of deeper green, a cord along which the color played, now light, now dark, rhythmically. The other end of that cord remained hidden. To see with the mind's eyes, Brixia had heard of that but had never really believed it could be done.

"Dwed!"

The cord snapped taut. There was a need to save— to draw— But no one could lay hand on this. For

where there was no physical body, neither did a hand exist.

Within herself Brixia fumbled, strove to master this new sense this awareness she had not known any could have—which she did not understand.

"Dwed!" Again that call in the other's voice—or thought.

Though the cord remained taut, there was no more movement in it. There must be a way! In the past Brixia had known times when she had driven her body to a point where flesh, bone, and blood had been exhausted close to death. Now—she must so drive this other part of her. This was like using a new tool or weapon, for which she had no training—only desperation and great need.

"Dwed!" That was her call this time. And it seemed as if the name itself wove about the cord, thickened and strengthened it. Out flowed the wave of another force, not hers. For a moment Brixia flinched from uniting with that. Then, knowing that only together might come victory, she surrendered.

Draw—draw back the cord, guide so Dwed's return! Be not only an anchorage holding him still to life, but prepare for him a road of escape.

The cord—in her vivid mental picture that was beginning to change. Small leaves of green-gold as brilliant as precious metal broke forth along it. Now it was a vine— Grow, pull—this way was life!

Thought closed about the vine in a grip as tight as willing hands might have. Draw—

"Dwed!"

Leaf by leaf the vine was moving, coming back and back. Pull!

"Dwed!"

The vine was gone—the cold, the dark broke like a bubble shattered from within. She was in the light once more, back in time and place. Dwed lay still in

Marbon's arms. The boy's face was very pale, the green light of the stone gave it an overcast like that of the touch of death.

"Dwed!" Marbon's hand cupped the boy's chin, raising his head.

There was a flutter of eyelashes. Dwed's lips parted in a slow sigh. Slowly the eyelids lifted. But the eyes were blank, unfocused.

"Cold—" he whispered faintly. A shudder shook his limp body. "So very cold—"

Brixia's hands shook as she still cupped the stone. On impulse, and because she felt she had hardly any strength left in her now to continue to hold it, she placed the Bane on Dwed's breast, brought up his flaccid hands to rub between her own. His flesh was clammy and chill.

"Dwed—" Marbon called his name loudly as the boy's eyes once more closed. "Do not leave us, Dwed!"

Again the boy sighed. His head turned a little on his lord's arm so that his face was half hidden.

"Dwed!" the name was now a cry of fear.

"He sleeps—he has not gone." Brixia fell back rather than moved away. "Truly he is with you again."

With you, she thought. Not with us. What part had she now in their lives?

"Only by your grace and favor, Wise Woman." Marbon settled the boy gently on the floor.

She had seen this man's face vacant, enraged, absorbed by the obsession of his quest. But now he looked very different somehow. She could not read the meaning behind his eyes. She was too tired, too drained in mind and body.

"I—am—no—Wise-woman—" She spoke slowly out of the overwhelming ache of that tiredness. Uta pressed against her, purring, rubbing her head along Brixia's arm in one of her most meaningful caresses.

The girl half put out her hand for the Bane, but she never completed that action. Instead a wave of darkness arose and swept her away.

Flowers around her, she lay in a scented nest of blossoms. Others hung from the branches which curtained her around. She could see only the pearl white of their petals, the carved perfection of them. Among them wound vines brightly green. Brixia thought drowsily that the rustling she heard was the whisper of flower and vine together.

Louder grew that whispering—and with it a murmur like the sweet plucking of lute strings. The flowers, the vines, sang:

> "Zarsthor's land fallow lies,
>   His fields stark bare.
> No man may guess in aftertime
>   Who held the lordship there.
> Thus by the shame of Eldor's pride
>   Death and ruin came to bide.
>
> The stars have swung—
>   The Time is ripe.
> They face once more
>   The doom of night.
> Broken now in dark and shame
>   Is the force of Zarsthor's Bane.
>
> Green grow the fields,
>   The circling hills.
> Lost in years past
>   All ancient ills.
> Who holds this land
>   Under the day,
> Will follow in peace
>   Another way."

Only jingling rhymes—no polished songsmith's lay.

The flowers swung to it, the vine leaves whispered and waved. Languidly Brixia closed her eyes, content to rest in this fragrant bed which was so far from labor, fear and pain. But through the song, the lute's murmur, a voice called imperiously:

"Brixia!"

> "Who holds this land
>   Under the day,
> Will follow in peace
>   Another way—"

"Brixia!"

Once more she opened her eyes. This was not her place of peace and flowers. She lay under the open sky. Under her, as her hands moved aimlessly, at her sides, was the softness of grass cut and heaped to make a bed. She was not alone. To her right Lord Marbon sat cross-legged, to her left was Dwed still white faced. Uta arose from by her feet, stretched and yawned.

Brixia frowned. Certainly she had not been here— no, rather in that domed place of the lake city—when last she remembered.

"You—did you sing that song?" she asked slowly, looking once more to Marbon.

"No." He shook his head. With his lips shaping such a smile she thought she could understand, seeing also that which dwelt in his eyes, softened his features, that tie which had led Dwed to follow and serve his stricken lord—even to the edge of death. If this man offered friendship it was a gift worth the taking.

"It was you who sang—in your sleep." He told her. "Or did you really wander in another place, lady, where dreams are more real and this life but a dream? Though I find the promise in your song good. 'Who holds the land under the day!' —who holds the land," he repeated softly as if he found in that a promise.

"What land, lord?" Dwed cut in.

"That which the Bane once destroyed, which is now free again. Look, lady, and see how your song comes true!"

Before Brixia could move Marbon was at her side, his arm slipped beneath her shoulders. He lifted her with a gentle concern which she had forgotten one of her kind might ever show to another. She needed his strength for her support for she felt very weak, as one who arouses after a serious illness.

So resting against him she looked beyond. Uta pranced in a circle about the growing spear of a plant. Grass lay in a waving, lush crown of green about that spear, taller, richer in color than that growing elsewhere. And, half way up that spear of shining red-brown there was a bulge in the bark.

Brixia had never seen growth in action before. Even as she watched that swelling on the trunk cracked, opened to release a pod also red-brown, perhaps the size of her little finger. While before her eyes that shoot which had given birth to the pod grew visibly taller, thicker, put out two branches, and still grew.

The fresh grass spread out in ripples of vivid green on and on from the roots of the plant, shooting up to replace the duller blades which had been there. There were now smaller pods on the two branches. This—this was a tree—a tree growing the sum of years' thickening, spreading, reaching, in only moments of their time!

"What—where—?" Brixia clutched at Marbon's nearer hand.

"It grows from the seed you brought out of An-Yak, lady. There we planted Zarsthor's Bane. But what springs from it is no longer evil. Green magic, Wise Woman."

She moved to shake her head, brushing so against his shoulder.

"I have told you—I am no Wise Woman." She was a little afraid now—afraid of anything she could not truly understand.

"One does not always choose power," he answered quietly. "That sometimes chooses you. Do you think that you could have plucked the flower of the White Heart had you not had within you that which green magic inclined to! I—I sought the Bane for its power, and that dark shadow over-reached me—for I am of Zarsthor's doomed House and what was evil for him could also root in me, even as this tree has rooted here, its past blackness and evil destroyed.

"You sought no power, so it was freely given to you in your need. Did not even the Bane lose its threat in your hands? What you wrought then—that was greater magic than any I could aspire to do."

Brixia shook her head again. "Not my doing—it was from the flower—also, it was in the end the choice of Eldor and Zarsthor—for when they came together in that place they had even forgotten what had tied them in hatred among the shadows."

She remembered the two worn men as she had seen them last, how they had answered the questions that someone, or something, perhaps even the Bane itself, had put in her mind to ask.

"Zarsthor?" He made a question of the name.

Brixia told him of the two who had demanded the Bane of her, and of how they had at last gone away together, free of the bonds their own acts had laid upon them.

"And you say you have no power?" Marbon marveled. "How it comes to one does not matter—how one uses it does."

The girl sat up, drawing away from his light hold. "I

do not want it!" she cried aloud to all about her—more to the unseen than to him, Dwed, or Uta.

Now the swift growing tree was more than a sapling, ever thickening branches hung lower, burdened as they were with more and more swelling buds. Even as Brixia voiced her denial the first and largest of the buds split its casing. A flower opened—white and perfect. Though it was day and the sun was out over their heads—still the flower was in bloom.

Brixia blinked and blinked again. There was no denying what she could so plainly see. Fruit of the Bane Marbon had said. Brixia bit her lip. The flower she had carried—which had withered away in that fog-land—had it given its life to this? She must accept that such things could be when the evidence stood before her eyes. New thoughts, awakening emotions stirred in her—they were both fascinating and frightening. Perhaps she had been marked for this task in some way on that first night when Kuniggod had brought her into the refuge of that place of the Old Ones—the place of quiet peace.

"What must I do then!" she asked in a small voice, wishing no answer, but knowing she must listen to one.

"Accept," Marbon stood up, his arms flung wide, his face raised to the sky. "This was the Bane killed land of Zarsthor. Perhaps it has lain too long under the shadow to truly awake again." He turned his head to look at the walls in the sunken lake basin. "An-Yak is gone. But one can build anew—"

For the second time Dwed spoke. "What of Eggarsdale then, my lord?"

Marbon shook his head slowly. "We cannot go back, foster son. Eggarsdale lies behind—both in distance and time. This now is ours—"

Brixia looked from him to the tree. That stood taller

than Marbon now. Unlike the one under which she had sheltered her first night in the Waste, the branches of this were not twisted nor interwoven among themselves, but lifted their tips upward, spread well apart from one another, as if to both welcome the clear sky and roof that portion of the earth covered with the thick fresh grass.

Theirs? Unconscious of what she did, she held out her right hand towards the tree. That first bloom to open broke from its stem. Though she felt no wind against her cheek, or ruffling her tousled hair, the flower drifted straightway to her, settled upon her hand. Did it come in answer to her unvoiced desire—even as Uta (when she chose, of course) would come to her call?

Theirs! Brixia cupped the flower and drew deep breaths of its fragrance. Like an outworn garment the past dropped from her. It was gone—the world was changed, even as Zarsthor's Bane had become this wondrous thing.